please send help...

ALSO BY
GABY DUNN & ALLISON RASKIN

i hate everyone but you

please send help...

GABY DUNN & ALLISON RASKIN

WEDNESDAY BOOKS
NEW YORK

First published in the United States by Wednesday Books, an imprint of St. Martin's Publishing Group

PLEASE SEND HELP. Copyright © 2019 by Gaby Dunn and Allison Raskin. All rights reserved. Printed in the United States of America. For information, address St. Martin's Press, 120 Broadway, New York, NY 10271.

www.wednesdaybooks.com

Designed by Anna Gorovoy

The Library of Congress Cataloging-in-Publication Data is available upon request.

ISBN 978-1-250-21653-3 (hardcover)
ISBN 978-1-250-21654-0 (ebook)

Our books may be purchased in bulk for promotional, educational, or business use. Please contact your local bookseller or the Macmillan Corporate and Premium Sales Department at 1-800-221-7945, extension 5442, or by email at MacmillanSpecialMarkets@macmillan.com.

First Edition: July 2019

10 9 8 7 6 5 4 3 2 1

TO EACH OTHER. LOVE YOU.

Sun, Sep 8, 5:42 PM EST

We're officially back in the same time zone!

But we're over a thousand miles apart

Why do you always see the negative?!

Because of my brain. And how it works.

Ah right. How could I forget?

Text me when you get to your apartment.

You mean the youth hostel?

GEN

JK. I got an apartment!

Thank god.

Do you think you'll ever stop being so gullible?

Maybe in my sixties!

No!

Seventies!

Can't wait 👍

COCKROACH, BEDBUGS, AND FLEAS OH MY

 Ava Helmer <AVA.HELMER@gmail.com>   9/8/19
to Gen

Dear Best* Friend,

I've officially scoured every inch of my brand-new (to me) N.Y.C. apartment and did not find a single bug, bug dropping or cobweb. Is it possible that I am the exception to the rule? Will I somehow survive my early twenties without finding la cucaracha in my bed? I better be. I might have beaten out hundreds of kids for this internship but I will pack up and go home to Cali the moment I feel something crawling on me.

Remember that time junior year of high school when that spider fell on my head during the only time I made out in high school???? And then you called me a Bug Queen while I cried? I think I finally have enough time and perspective to find that hilarious now.
(*Memories . . . Makes me feel fine!* FYI that was to the tune of *Summer breeze . . . Makes me feel fine.*)

My roomie/co-intern still isn't here even though we both start at 7AM tomorrow. I took the bigger room at first, but then felt bad and moved into the smaller one. Why do I do this to myself? Unclear, my dear friend, unclear!

I can't believe I'm officially an adult. I mean I have zero income and no social life to speak of but I officially go to "work" now instead of "school." Did you ever think we'd make it this far when we were fourteen and I was still figuring out how to properly shave my armpit hair without cutting myself? I sure didn't! We don't even live on the West Coast anymore! Life is crazy! (I know you haven't really lived on the West Coast for four years, but I've always been a late bloomer.) At this rate I should have a husband and kids by forty-five! Anything is possible!

Speaking of the impossible becoming possible . . .

Mind the Gap with Halona McBride!!

I get to work on _Mind the Gap with Halona McBride_!! The greatest show on television! The _only_ prime-time late-night show on television with a female host! But I don't have to tell you that. Because I already told you all summer long. (Thank you again for coming back to L.A. to pretty much exclusively hang out with me. I needed one last summer with my BFF. Plus you'd outgrown Boston/Emerson anyway. I like to think I outgrew USC after my third semester . . .)

Wow. I'm sweating. What do you think Halona McBride smells like? Will I get close enough to smell her? My thoughts are spinning!

I know it's only 8PM but I want to go to bed. I guess I have to wait for Dana to get here so she doesn't think I'm a freak who goes to bed at 8PM regularly. (I only do it on school nights.)

TELL ME ABOUT YOUR APARTMENT! IS IT INSIDE A SWAMP?!

Xoxoxooxoxoxoxoxoxoxoxoxoxoxoxoxoxoxoxoxoxoxoxoxoxoxo xoxoxoxoxoxoxoxoxoxox

Ava

*Oldest, Favorite, Most Queer, Loudest Friend

Re: COCKROACH, BEDBUGS, AND FLEAS OH MY

 Gen Goldman <GEN.GOLDMAN@gmail.com>   9/8/19
to Ava

Hi!! Sorry to reply so late. I hope you're asleep by now since it's well past 9PM. My apartment is infested with alligators and mosquitos. I've made them my pets. I named one after you. She's very pretty . . .

Turns out Florida is HOT! And not in a good way. My pits have been dripping since we touched down. I can't tell if not shaving them has made it better or worse. (The smell is definitely worse.)

Turns out, my apartment is right by the airport. So I can escape at the drop of a hat if it turns out journalism isn't for me.

JUST KIDDING! I am clearly following my dream of upholding the fourth estate by writing for a failing Southern newspaper. *The Fernandina Beach Centennial* will rise from its grave on my hardworking back! Or I'll quit and start blogging my diet like most of my former classmates. And your grandma thought I wouldn't amount to anything!

My studio apartment is surprisingly big for $650 a month, but I guess that's the cost of no living. I don't have any furniture, so I'm gonna sleep on the floor tonight and figure out my interior design vision tomorrow. I'm thinking tacky yet beachy.

Okay, ta ta for now. I have one hundred hours of *Forensic Files* to catch up on.

TITS & ASS

Gen

Mon, Sep 9, 5:30 AM
🌀 FIRST DAY OF WORK!
🌀 DANA IS A BOY!
🌀 MY LIFE IS CRAZY!

6:45 AM
🌀 First one here. Building is locked.

6:48 AM
🌀 Door was not locked. Security guy was watching me struggle the whole time. Mortifying.

6:55 AM

Remember when I thought the door was locked?!

No one else is here.

8:35 AM

Dana's a dude????

How hot?

1 to 10

9:35 AM

Smart on you for taking some time to think about it. I eagerly await your response re: Dana's hotness.

10:35 AM

I bought a water bed.

Florida has changed me.

DANA IS AN 8.5

 Ava Helmer <AVA.HELMER@gmail.com>   9/9/19
to Gen

Hi! Sorry I didn't text back! Today was INSANE. By the time all the interns arrived (7:15ish because I guess no one cares about call times), we were nonstop until 5.

This guy, Ben, is our supervisor so he showed us the ropes, which was basically a long list of what not to do. Dana says Ben is pretty big in the N.Y. stand-up scene. He did have a lot of one-liners about Halona's mood swings. I hope this is just a case of a man thinking a woman is hysterical because she's not smiling and not an actual case of Bipolar II. (Mood swings are very debilitating.)

I didn't get to see Halona since we're still technically on hiatus. For a female-run show, there are a lot of dudes running around.

How did I not realize Dana was a boy? He never used exclamation points when we were trying to find an apartment. I should have known.

I don't want to be a total PRUDE but I'm supposed to share a bathroom with a guy? And not just any guy, a straight, good-looking dude who went to Harvard? Shoot me in the fucking face.

All the interns are about to get pizza. There are ten of us in total. Most of them seem unimpressive, which makes me feel unimpressive. Hopefully we will all open up and blossom. Or, they will close off and die and I'll be the last (wo)man standing!

I'm think I'm gonna get onions on my pizza! No one can control me anymore!

A

P.S. I probably won't get onions.

Re: DANA IS AN 8.5

 Gen Goldman <GEN.GOLDMAN@gmail.com>   9/9/19
to Ava

Did you get onions or not?! I'm on the edge of my seat!

Glad everything went well today. If they ever pit the interns against each other in a *Hunger Games*–type scenario, it sounds like you would win!

Here is a list of what I've accomplished today:

1) Bought a water bed

2) Jumped on water bed

3) Bought used sheets (don't yell at me)

4) Decided to run for local office

5) Looked into running for local office, decided against it

6) Bought groceries like a GD ADULT (cereal and milk)

I'm meeting with my editor tomorrow. I've already found out everything there is to know about him. LIKE YOU SHOULD HAVE DONE WITH DANA! How did you not even Instagram stalk your future roommate??? Have I taught you nothing??

Grady Adams, editor-in-chief of *The Fernandina Beach Centennial,* was born and raised five miles from his place of work. His wife, Bambi, is a homemaker who spends her free time protesting abortion clinics. They have two children, one of whom works as a copy editor at the newspaper with Pops. The other has been in and out of rehab, but has recently "found Jesus" and now sells homemade crucifixes on the beach.

I THINK IT'S PRETTY CLEAR I'M GOING TO FIT RIGHT IN!

While I was able to find Grady Adams's property value, I was unable to find out anything about Jacksonville's gay scene online. I guess that is one thing I will need to research IRL. How hard can it be? Every city has a gay scene, even if it's secret and underground. (Oh! I hope it's secret and underground! Everything is more fun when it's a secret!)

Do you think it's too much if I wear a tie *and* Timberlands tomorrow? Or should I ease them in to my gender fluidity?

My right side is covered in mosquito bites. They must really hate lefties down here.

GAYYYYY,

Gen

11:56 PM

I DIDN'T GET ONIONS

Why are you still awake??? Have you been kidnapped?

No! I've been "partying."

This doesn't sound like Ava at all! Who is this?!

Boy Byeeeeee

I've had one cider.

Tue, Sep 10, 5:35 AM

I regret everything.

8:45 AM

Are you hurt?

Stop talking so loud. My head is pounding.

Sugary drinks will kill you. Life lesson 404.

Are you excited for your first day of work????

I was until I learned about Fernandina Beach's concealed carry law.

Is that better or worse than Stand Your Ground?

Depends if you own a gun or not.

Send help.

Help.

FIVE PEOPLE WORK HERE

 Gen Goldman <GEN.GOLDMAN@gmail.com>   9/10/19

to Ava

And two of them are members of the same family (the ADAMS family lol).

I showed up at 9:07 sharp and found Beau Adams, 31, playing snake on a computer. (How? I don't know.)

The rest of the staff, Grady, Floyd, Phyllis and the photographer Saul were all out covering a local baseball game. Why did they all need to cover it? Hard to say.

When they came back around lunch they looked at me like I was a very bad burglar. I honestly think Grady forgot he hired me. Once I jogged his decomposing memory, he lit up like an evangelical Christmas tree and pointed at a computer like an ape who wants a banana. (Wow, I'm overloading on the similes. Don't tell any of my professors.)

Anyway, your girl is officially in charge of bringing *The Fernandina Beach Centennial* to the web. I mean it's already on the web, but the interface is inscrutable. Like it looks like they just scanned a hard copy of the paper and then just posted the PDF? The type is very tiny.

I tried to explain (again) that I'm a journalist and not a web designer but Grady assumes all of Gen Z knows how to use Photoshop and control driverless cars with their minds.

This place is ridiculous, but it's the only place that was going to give me a full-time reporting job with a staff writer title. I'll get a few crocodile-based bylines here and then head out for greener pastures (like an actual city).

Maybe I'll uncover some crazy shit. Small towns keep big secrets. Fingers crossed I'm sitting on a hotbed of violence and corruption!

Remember to drink at least one glass of water to combat that one cider.

Gen

Re: FIVE PEOPLE WORK HERE

 Ava Helmer <AVA.HELMER@gmail.com>   9/10/19
to Gen

Thank you for your professional medical advice. I will take your suggestion strongly under advisement.

I'm actually feeling a lot better. I think I was just sleepy? My body is used to AT LEAST nine hours a night!

I googled *The Fernandina Beach Centennial* to make sure you weren't just fucking with me. I found a staff photo. WOW those people love Crocs. Please don't take offense, but why did these people hire you??? Was it your exposé for the *Globe* on gerrymandering or your takedown of sexual harassment in candlepin bowling leagues? (Still afraid of Boston, for the record.)

What's Beau like? Is he as "retro" as his dad?

I'd write more, but I think I'm supposed to be doing something. I'm just not sure what. . . .

Your undervalued intern,

Ava

7:35 PM

How many nights in a row am I allowed to eat fast food alone before it becomes "sad"?

No nights.

They have salad in Florida.

Journalists don't have time for salads! We eat on the go.

Where are you going?

Nowhere fast.

10:35 PM

Do you think my roommate relationship with Dana would survive if one of us saw the other one naked by accident?

You saw him naked???

No!

He saw you naked?!

Unclear.

Nice. Lucky guy.

I SAW HER

 Ava Helmer <AVA.HELMER@gmail.com>   9/11/19
to Gen

Halona McBride is real. I know because I saw her with my own eyes. She looks exactly like she does on TV except maybe for her height, weight and hair color. We didn't make eye contact or anything but I can tell we are going to have a special connection.

(I'm kidding. Please don't call my therapist and tell her I'm having psychotic delusions. Again.)

It was very brief. She was in and out before heading to some huge meeting. Intern boss Ben says she's lost weight because she's going through a divorce. I have no idea how he knows this stuff. Maybe they're super close?

I've spent the last three hours going through news footage to see who looks the dumbest. It's a tough job but someone has to do it!

I also did a coffee run. Apparently, I just need to know how to order it not make it. Another summer lost learning how to French press! At least I didn't get sunburned!

A

Re: I SAW HER

 Gen Goldman <GEN.GOLDMAN@gmail.com>   9/11/19
to Ava

Have you seen her husband?? There is no way she would let him go!

I'm glad you finally saw her and now know for certain she isn't just a high-tech hologram. She looked otherworldly at the White House Correspondents' dinner.

Sorry about the wasted coffee experience. I'm sure it will pay off the next time you're between writing jobs and have to moonlight as a barista. That's an integral part of the journey from what I've seen on TV.

Do you think you'll get to pitch jokes? Or is it not that kind of internship? Seems like a waste if not, since you sent such an intense writing sample. I still laugh thinking about Obama as the actual second coming. HOW DID WE NOT REALIZE!

Things are really heating up over here. Grady told me I could cover a school board meeting but then he took it back. Apparently I don't know enough about the subtleties of Fernandina Beach politics yet. I'm pretty sure they love guns and hate sex education. What else is there to know?

Right now I'm trying to learn web design from YouTube videos. Wish me luck.

P.S. Do you think they will notice if I turn the newspaper into a Tumblr account?

7:15 PM

I think they would notice.

Notice what?

If you turned the website into a Tumblr.

Too late. It's been four hours and no one has said anything.

GEN!

JK. Tumblr is too good for Fernandina Beach.

What are you doing?

Staying late with Ben to learn how to use the copier.

Sounds like the start of a really boring porn . . .

He's my boss!

Classic porn.

Good luck coding.

FU

Re: SYSTEMS BACK ONLINE

 Gen Goldman <GEN.GOLDMAN@gmail.com>   9/13/19
to Ava

Sorry, I was MIA yesterday. I spent all day reading back issues of *The Fernandina Beach Centennial.* This city is crazy! The mayor went to jail for domestic violence. And then BECAME THE MAYOR. Four years ago, the fire department got in trouble for hoarding all the cats they rescued from trees. (It was twenty-nine cats. They had twenty-nine cats.)

I thought this place would be boring, but I'm pretty sure if I do the most basic investigating I will uncover a whole herd of illegal chickens somewhere.

After seven hours of learning why it's important to not pay taxes but still be able to collect welfare, I decided I needed human interaction. I asked Beau where the younger locals go to unwind and he replied, "I go to my aunt's house." At first I thought he was inviting me to his aunt's house, but thankfully he was not. So I ventured out on my own.

The first place I saw on "Main Street" was called "GOTCHA." And boy did they get me. I had three beers in thirty minutes. Don't worry, they were only $2 each. I think they were homemade? Better not to know.

I chatted up the bartender for a bit. She was sort of cool . . .

Actually, looking back, she was the worst, but she was under thirty so we felt like kindred spirits at the time.

I think I might need to download a dating app. Here's hoping this town has Wi-Fi. (Or any queer people.)

Re: SYSTEMS BACK ONLINE

 Ava Helmer <AVA.HELMER@gmail.com>   9/13/19
to Gen

Hi! I didn't even realize we didn't talk! I've been so frazzled. Seven hours of sleep is NOT enough for me.

$2 beer seems very dangerous for you. I think I might call GOTCHA and ask them to charge you $5.

I'm sorry you haven't made friends just yet. Are there any colleges nearby? Maybe Beau's aunt is cooler than you think?

I think what you need is a big story! Remember when you uncovered a huge sexual harassment scandal the first MONTH of college? There has to be something fishy in Fernandina Beach! (Pun intended.)

Dana and I are getting along surprisingly well given my history with roommates. And with men.

My entire suite from sophomore year has still blocked me on Instagram. JOKE'S ON YOU! I can see anything from a web browser.

Dana has a crush on one of the segment producers, Jenna. She's at least thirty-five. And married to a woman. I actually think he has a chance though. I'll be sure to keep you updated.

We've discussed buying a second couch together. Things are getting PRETTY serious.

My parents are calling me multiple times a day. How the tables have turned! Who is codependent now! (It's still me but now also my mom.)

I totally forgot to answer your question re: pitching jokes. The answer is generally no, but they love to dangle the carrot. Ben says if I think of anything really great I should tell him and he will pass it on on my behalf. I think I have a crush on Ben. Anyway, I have to get back to the "grind." These office supplies won't deliver themselves.

Vaarwel!

Ava
(Remember when we studied abroad in Amsterdam?! That was pretty cool.)

9:15 PM

CAUGHT!

Oh, no!

You thought I wouldn't see it?

I was hoping.

I've long suspected you skim my emails.

HOW DARE YOU!

I always ctrl-F "crush"

And "sex"

And "Gen"

Ha! I should have known.

So. Spill.

Nothing to spill. Just a harmless little
crush on an authority figure.

Ew.

That's my thing.

Check your email in like thirty minutes

Why?

9:37 PM

Why?

9:45 PM

I'm scared.

A BRIEF HISTORY OF BAD IDEAS

 Gen Goldman <GEN.GOLDMAN@gmail.com>   9/13/19

to Ava

Below is an incomplete list of your misguided romantic
infatuations.

1) Jake Something Or Other: Freshman year of
college. Mean frat guy who couldn't act. Gave your PIV
virginity to him. Broke up after only a few months.
Ignored you on campus for two and a half years.

2) Aaron Rodriguez: Second half of freshman year. You spent months pining over him even though it was clear he was not interested. Very humiliating. Hard to recover from.

3) Jessie Weisman: Three summer "flings" in a row. Each time you thought you two would stay together during the school year. Each time, you did not. Would not return your calls from August to May. You claimed to be "in love."

4) Matt Lewis: Your TA! You hypocrite!

5) Painter guy senior year. Can't remember his name. Doubt he remembers yours.

6) Ben. Your boss.

Just some food for thought! Have a great night!

Gen

Re: A BRIEF HISTORY OF BAD IDEAS

 Ava Helmer <AVA.HELMER@gmail.com>   9/13/19
to Gen

UNSUBSCRIBE

(Thanks for not mentioning Johannes. That one still hurts.)

Re: A BRIEF HISTORY OF BAD IDEAS

 Gen Goldman <GEN.GOLDMAN@gmail.com>   9/13/19
to Ava

Fuck! I forgot Johannes. That guy really screwed you.
Thank god the embassy got you ANOTHER
PASSPORT.

Sat, Sep 14, 8:15 AM
Why am I awake?

8:35 AM
Are you awake?

9:21 AM
Have you ever seen the Today show?
These people are crazy.
Who hired them?

9:42 AM
Hi! Sorry! Slept in!
I have seen the Today show. It is not
good.

😳 I am so bored. Can you come visit me?

😐 Sure. How about Columbus Day?

😳 When is that?

😐 October.

😳 But I'm bored NOW!

😐 Go swimming in the ocean.

😳 Are you threatening me?

SO I WENT TO THE BEACH . . .

 Gen Goldman <GEN.GOLDMAN@gmail.com>   9/15/19

to Ava

And I found a WHALE of a TALE! (Thank you, thank you very much.)

Where to begin! I know: my outfit!

I wanted to "blend in" with the locals so I wore my dad's rattiest Hawaiian shirt and cutoff jeans. I looked hot yet approachable. I set up camp near a volleyball game in the hopes of getting hit on the head and taken out of my misery of living in Florida.

Instead, the ball simply rolled into my lap and a star was born. Turns out, I am VERY good at volleyball. Full disclosure, I was playing against fifteen-year-olds, but some of them were very tall.

The whole group of teens go to this charter school, West Lake. Remember the name West Lake.

Let me tell you about West Lake. It's a shit show.
They're funded by the government but have almost no
oversight. Every few months the parents of the
students have to "donate" a couple hundred bucks to
keep the school going. (Yes, this is illegal.)

But that's not even the craziest part. Joanne, the
second tallest, told me that on the second Saturday of
every month, the school administration turns the gym
into an underground nightclub, sells alcohol without a
license and charges an entrance fee.

GUESS WHAT YESTERDAY WAS:

That's right. The second Saturday of the month!

I think it's obvious what happened next. I infiltrated the
illegal nightclub with the help of my new teenage
friends! Hijinks ensued!

Well, not really. But they did tell me where to go and
how to get in. They couldn't attend because they are
clearly underage and attend the school. So old Gen
was flying solo on her first sting of the year.

It was surprisingly easy to get in. I just had to pay ten
dollars and say "Marlin." I'm starting to think I didn't
even need a password and those kids were just
fucking with me . . .

NEVERTHELESS, SHE PERSISTED

I was in. I think they used the term "nightclub" a little
too loosely, but it definitely charged at the door and

sold alcohol. There was heterosexual debauchery all around me! A lot of low-cut blouses with crucifix necklaces bouncing between exposed breasts. . . . (Should I write erotica? Yes or no?)

I only stayed for an hour or so after talking to a few "regulars" who confirmed this was indeed a monthly occurrence. I was on my way out when I bumped into this girl who I later learned was named Coralee. I only learned this because after we went to GOTCHA together, I asked her what her tattoo meant and she said, "It's my name."

Coralee is our age and *just* broke up with her high school boyfriend. So it's the perfect time for me to swoop in and steal her heart.

Overall, I had a pretty great day. Uncovered a scam. Met my first wife. Learned how to spike.

WHAT DID YOU DO?

G

P.S. I am very burnt. I need you here to remind me to wear sunscreen.

Re: SO I WENT TO THE BEACH . . .

Ava Helmer <AVA.HELMER@gmail.com>   9/15/19
to Gen

Wow! Lot to unpack here. My thoughts below in no particular order.

1) You can buy sunblock that smells really good. Coconut or mango. I think if it smells good you will want to eat it and then when you realize you can't eat it you will still want it on your body.

2) You are not good at volleyball. Every few years you think that you are good at volleyball. I have seen you play many times. Grunting the loudest is not part of the actual game.

3) Is Coralee bi? Does she have any experience with women? Will this be straight-girl-Leslie all over again?

4) CONGRATULATIONS! You have cracked a case! It is a strange case that could probably only happen in Florida, but it is a case nonetheless!

5) I hope you washed your dad's shirt. He has done some filthy things.

On a less beachy note, I have survived my first week of work AND half a weekend. I think I'm an official New Yorker now. I really thought I would have flown home crying by now. (No need to list all the times I have flown home crying. They are seared into my brain.)

I really like it here. Dana is a surprisingly good roommate and work goes by quickly even though it's all menial tasks. We walked through Central Park yesterday and it felt like the beginning of a movie that won't really have enough conflict but is still enjoyable in the theater. (You would probably turn it off if you were watching at home though.)

We were going to go to the MET after but then realized no one actually wanted to go. We just thought we *should* go to seem cultured and sophisticated. I suggested ice cream instead and everyone (Dana, Ben, and this other intern Lacie) agreed. I'm basically the ringleader of the group now LOL. There must be a glitch in the Matrix.

Okay, I have to run because Dana wants to sign up for a UCB class and I said I'd check out the theater with him.

Is it weird I genuinely don't want to sleep with Dana? I would be mad if I found out he didn't want to sleep with me. Just because of the male sex drive etc. . . .

GOT TO GO! BUY SOME ALOE!

A

P.S. I think you are too niche to write mainstream erotica.

2:13 PM

Who said anything about MAINSTREAM erotica??

I want to have a strange but dedicated following!

Ha! Okay.

Strange in any specific way or . . .

Butt stuff.

Isn't that pretty mainstream at this point?

AVA!

You little hussy!

Why was Ben hanging out with you guys?

Ouch!

I've been working on my personality!

No! I mean why is the boss hanging out with the interns.

Oh. We were all talking about the park on Friday and it just sort of happened. He sort of planned the whole thing.

Send me a picture of him.

No.

Does he look like a person who has friends?

Hard to say, he does have claws and blood dripping from his mouth at all times.

FU I will google.

8:45 PM

He looks like he'd have 2 or 3 friends.

CODE RED

 Gen Goldman <GEN.GOLDMAN@gmail.com>   9/16/19

to Ava

Unbelievable. Or should I say: TOO FUCKING BELIEVABLE.

I waltz into Grady's office today, swag in my step, great story in my pocket. I plop into his wicker chair reserved for "guests" and tell him everything. My volleyball skills. The teens. The rave. The illegal alcohol sales. Everything. I have notes. I have photos. And . . .

HE LAUGHS.

For about two minutes. I think there were a few tears. Apparently this is the worst kept secret since Mrs. Norman's affair with her gardener (I have no idea who Mrs. Norman is btw). No one cares it's an illegal rave because it's good for the school. Don't I support education?!

At this point my blood is boiling. A few years ago I would have snapped that chair over his sweaty head, but instead, I muttered some RUDE things under my breath and walked out. Phyllis asked what happened and in a moment of weakness I told her. So SHE started laughing. Apparently the principal of West Lake is Grady's former brother-in-law and now cousin-in-law. You'd think he'd want this guy to go down! He left his sister for his cousin!

I don't know what to do. This is a great title but I can't waste my best years at a paper that won't let me report. I want to quit. Please talk me down.

G

Re: CODE RED

 Ava Helmer <AVA.HELMER@gmail.com>   9/16/19
to Gen

Can I say something "crazy" and "out of character"? I actually think you SHOULD quit. This job sucks. I never fully understood why you took it in the first place . . . You should be in a major city. There have to be other journalism jobs out there. I know you can't afford to do an internship but there has to be a better option than sweaty Grady in bumfuck Florida!

Come stay with me for a little! Dana and I have *quite* a soft couch. Oh my god! It will be so fun! I can't guarantee it, but maybe Dana will have sex with you??? He will probably have sex with you.

Just make sure you quit in epic Gen-like fashion! We want to really be able to milk this story for years to come!

A

Re: CODE RED

 Gen Goldman <GEN.GOLDMAN@gmail.com> 9/16/19
to Ava

I can't quit, Ava. You clearly don't understand my
situation. At all.

3:15 PM

Now you're mad at me???

You love to quit things!

You're the one who suggested quitting!

I don't have rich parents, Ava.

Okay . . .

I know that.

Do you?

Because big cities cost money.

And journalists don't make any.

That's not true! There are journalists
everywhere.

I'm not saying you have to move to N.Y.,
but this isn't your only option.

I can't quit after one week.

Who would hire me?

And I can't not work.

I have student loans. Unlike some
people.

Wow.

I'm sorry I don't have student loans and
that I want you to be happy.

I'm clearly a horrible person.

You're not horrible. You're out of touch.

Okay. BRB while I go watch Fox News.

Wed, Sep 18, 10:13 AM

Beau just told me he stabs frogs on the road and then eats them.

Also I forgive you.

I don't remember apologizing.

It was implied.

What do you mean he stabs them?

Or do I not want to know?

He stabs them with a rod and cooks them.

My life was fine before knowing this.

Sure, fine but not great.

True!

THE SHOW MUST GO ON

Ava Helmer <AVA.HELMER@gmail.com>   9/18/19
to Gen

Halona McBride is a B.I.T.C.H. And you know I use that term extremely lightly. But this time it's justified. She just threw what I can only describe as a tantrum because we didn't book the guests she wanted for next week.

Here's the crazy(est) part: she didn't tell anyone who she wanted for next week! She just assumed the booker would know??? Anyway, said booker is now fired, and no one got to eat lunch because she made us listen to some sort of speech that she was clearly pulling out of her ass in real time.

Some takeaways from said speech:

1) There is a reason we all deserve to be here. Also, we can be replaced at any time.

2) David Letterman would never have to put up with this shit.

3) She is a mom. (For some reason, she kept repeating that she is a mom. Apparently that is a VERY big deal and not something 80 percent of women do.)

4) We are not the news. We are more important than the news.

5) She's lost weight and no one has noticed.

They always say, don't meet your heroes. Imagine being yelled at by one!

We made eye contact briefly. I hope she likes me.

Ava

P.S. I now understand how people like Hitler came to power.

6:45 PM

I'm so sad about Halona.

Are you sure you weren't hallucinating due to N.Y.C. pollution?

You think I'm happy about this???

She was my hero!

Maybe she really is going through a divorce???

She threw a shoe at someone.

WHO?

No one knows! They were just passing by!

Here's a question. Would we all be so shocked and outraged at her behavior if she was a man?

If he threw a shoe? Yes.

You should see her clothes though. Flawless.

OMG, I bet.

THE GREATEST LOVE STORY EVER TOLD

 Gen Goldman <GEN.GOLDMAN@gmail.com>   9/19/19
to Ava

I have never met a girl like Coralee. I have never met a girl named Coralee. I want to bone Coralee.

I texted her after work last night and suggested meeting up for a drink. I thought enough time had passed since the rave where I would seem interested but not desperate. She wrote back immediately. I love flirting with straight women. They have no idea it's even happening until I have their shirt off!

We met up at my new favorite bar, GOTCHA, Fernandina Beach's number-one destination for warm beer and watered-down shots. I was wearing a plaid button-down and those jeans that make it look like I have a butt. She wore a short dress and cowboy boots.

Apparently, I LOVE a woman in cowboy boots.

It was awkward at first because she's never been to California or read a book, but once I found out she liked procedurals we were off to the races. No one knows more about crime shows than me. She likes *NCIS* the best, but I'm trying to look past her flaws. I'm sure she'll change her tune when I introduce her to *The Fall*. She will *fall* right into my arms. (I can hear you groaning from here.)

I decided two drinks in to take it slow. She's fresh off a breakup and has no idea that I'm what she clearly wants/needs. The girl was still wearing her class ring. . . . She has no idea what's good for her.

I forgot how fun it is to have a crush. I feel like I've been celibate for half my life. (Fifteen days and counting.) I think I judged this place too quickly. If there are just two or three more Coralees around, I should be set for a whole year!

She kissed my cheek at the end of the night. Real sensual like. She smells like Bath & Body Works's *Country Apple*.

Things are coming up Goldman!

G

Re: THE GREATEST LOVE STORY EVER TOLD

 Ava Helmer <AVA.HELMER@gmail.com>   9/19/19
to Gen

Coralee sounds like a fake name. Miss Coralee, your sweet tea is ready! Miss Coralee, the soldiers, they're a comin, from the North! Miss Coralee, are you friends with any black people?

Sorry. Sorry. I'm tired. And clearly judgemental about the South.

I'm glad you have a crush. I hope it turns into something true and fulfilling. Or you guys hook up a few times and stay really good friends. (Like most lesbians.)

Have you heard from Alex at all? Is he liking D.C.? What is he doing there again?

I wish I was still friends with one of my exes.

JUST KIDDING! I hate them all!

P.S. Dana definitely saw me naked that one time because he brought it up today in a big group and I had to laugh like I knew it was a thing that was okay. I hope he only saw the left nip. We both know the right one has some explaining to do.

6:45 PM

I don't know what my esteemed ex-boyfriend is doing.

We're not speaking.

What happened this time?

He insulted my intelligence.

Did he really? Or did you misinterpret something?

Are YOU insulting my intelligence?!

No! Never!

Good.

If there is one thing I know, it's when I've been insulted.

Or if someone is giving me bedroom eyes.

And that's why I never look you directly in the face.

7:13 PM

I bet Dana's jerked off to you.

Who is this??

hahahahahaha

BM SOS

 Ava Helmer <AVA.HELMER@gmail.com>   9/20/19
to Gen

Dearest Genevieve,

I write to you from a state of complete despair. The clock reads 11:45AM. I am hunched over my desk, in crippling pain for something horrible has happened:

My morning excrement did not come.

You know I adhere to a very strict schedule, especially when it comes to my bowels. But for some unforeseen reason, the poop would not come. Until now. While I am at work. And there is only one unisex bathroom. That is always busy.

This is hell. I am in hell.

If this massive shit kills me, promise not to tell anyone. Just tell them I loved too hard.

Good-bye forever,

Ava Helmer

11:52 AM
Just go to the bathroom!
I can't! Everyone will hear me!

Do you need me to get you that book
Everybody Poops?

No.

I already have three copies.

I think I might pass out from the exertion
of holding everything in.

Is it possible to give yourself a hernia?

AVA

Go to the bathroom! It's 2019!

You can't use that for this!

I can use it for everything!

I don't need to wear a bra! It's 2019!

Women can be professional baseball
players! It's 2019!

I wasn't going over the speed limit
because there is no speed limit! It's
2019!

Have you ever pooped at work?

Fuck no.

But you know I go at night.

12:13 PM

Greetings from my apartment.

I went home sick.

SO YOU COULD POOP?!

Don't judge me!

Women can be women however they
want!

It's 2019!

POSSIBLE SOLUTION

 Gen Goldman <GEN.GOLDMAN@gmail.com> 9/21/19
to Ava

What if I went behind Grady's back and tried to take the charter school story to a larger paper that isn't full of corruption? Like the *Miami Herald*? Or *The Florida Times Union*?? I bet they would be all over a story like this.

I have made a list of pros and cons so you won't ask me to.

PROS
• Corruption will be exposed
• Changes will be made
• I'll get a major byline

CONS
• The school will lose money and might have to shut down
• Grady will never trust me again, and I actually like Grady
• I will definitely, 100 percent, get fired

Tough call, I know. Leaning toward blowing this whole thing up.

SPEAK NOW OR FOREVER REGRET MY MISTAKES

G

TERRIBLE SOLUTION

 Ava Helmer <AVA.HELMER@gmail.com>   9/21/19
to Gen

Gen. Genevieve. Genny?

I think you must already know this is a bad idea because you're bothering to ask me. And your sign-off included the phrase "my mistakes."

Look, you'll be the first to tell me I'm no journalist, but this seems like the wrong move for multiple reasons.

1) No one will hire you after this because they won't be able to trust you. Remember last summer when you got drunk and started screaming about the importance of paper loyalty until that Target employee asked you to leave? What you are proposing is the opposite of that.

2) Is this story even worth it? No one is forcing these people to pay for the rave. What would you even be exposing? An illegal liquor license? Unapproved fun? If this was something that was actively hurting people I would tell you to do anything to get it out there, but it seems like a victimless crime that actually helps the school.

3) Shouldn't you use this rebellious spirit to find a better story? One that actually needs to be exposed?

I hope you are very impressed with my moral relativism. I plan to bring it up for years to come!

A

P.S. Ben just texted me "hey" on a weekend.

Re: TERRIBLE SOLUTION

 Gen Goldman <GEN.GOLDMAN@gmail.com>   9/21/19
to Ava

I see what you did with that subject-line change. Well played.

Ugh. I guess you're right. AS ALWAYS. I shall disregard this flagrant disrespect for the law in lieu of a better story. (If I don't find one though I'm gonna burn that party to the ground.)

On a lighter note, Ben definitely wants to fuck.

6:23 PM

Why would you say that??

It's not like he wrote "U UP"

That part was implied.

He sent the text in the morning!

Ever heard of day drinking?

What did you write back?

I haven't yet.

AVA!

What? I didn't know what to say.

Now he's going to fall in love with you!!

Why?! Because I didn't text him back?

Yes.

Duh.

I'll just write back now.

What are you wearing?

Um. My lavender Splendid dress and tights.

Good, because I have a feeling you'll be wearing that tomorrow too.

HOW DID YOU KNOW?

 Ava Helmer <AVA.HELMER@gmail.com>   9/22/19
to Gen

Seriously. Do you have powers? Are you a soothsayer? You can tell me. I promise not to turn you in to the government. Unless they really need you.

I spent the night with Ben. NOT the way you think. But also a little bit the way you think.

After our convo, I spent another thirty minutes figuring out the perfect response and decided on "Hey!" He immediately replied, making me think it might be a work thing, but he asked what I was doing. Apparently he had an extra ticket to a screening of *Funny Girl* at the Film Forum. I had to leave right away in order to meet him, which was good because it didn't really give me time to think about what I was doing. YOU KNOW WHAT HAPPENS WHEN I LET MYSELF THINK!

He was waiting for me outside wearing what I can only describe as female catnip: white Converse, no socks, button-down, tight jeans. WOOF! (Sorry for barking.)

I didn't know if I should hug him or not so I shook his hand. Yep. I shook his hand even though he is someone I already spend 5 out of 7 days with. He laughed and assumed I was being charming. (Thank god for Zooey Deschanel.)

The movie was wonderful and then terrible. Why do people feel the need to ruin a perfectly happy story with a sad ending? (Yes, I am aware this is a biopic but they could have kept it to the good stuff like they did with that Stephen Hawking movie. That couple didn't make it IRL but no one needs to know that! Not me!)

I thought I would head home after the movie, but Ben wanted to get ice cream. That's right. Ice cream. Not a drink. A dessert. I didn't know life could be so fun!

We shared two cones (four flavors) and walked around a bit. I felt like a modern-day princess when he opened a door for me. My expectations are way too low. But I'm young and in love with my supervisor! It's a tale as old as time!

I think you would actually like Ben. He's very sarcastic and smart. He's read almost as much fiction as I have AND he doesn't know how to fix anything with his hands. So he is clearly not a slave to the gender binary!

I ended up back at his place. It took me a while to figure out he had been guiding us there the whole time. Probably because he acted surprised too, like, "Oh, this is actually my place. Want to see it?" I did want to see it!

He lives alone, which makes him a god among men in Manhattan. (I think he must have rich parents. Is it bad that I like the idea of my significant other having rich parents?) The place is decorated like someone other than a single thirty something man decorated it. Far too many accessories.

I still wasn't sure if we were on a "date" or if he was just a friendly guy who wanted someone to hang out with on a Saturday night because his normal friends were out of town. I mean fine, he invited me to a movie, navigated me into his place, and put on smooth jazz, but maybe he just wanted to keep it platonic! (I know. I know. I have low self-esteem. But I still find it shocking whenever someone is physically attracted to me. We're in New York! There are models here!)

We were talking about his sketch team (which he does on top of stand-up) and he showed me a few videos. They are pretty funny! I mean not like LOL but not unbearable? He looks very cute on-camera.

After about an hour he asked me if I wanted to go home. This caused me to panic and assume I had far overstayed my welcome. I jumped up and grabbed my things, apologizing for staying so late; I had clearly misunderstood what was going on. He grabbed my arm at that point and assured me he didn't want me to leave. He just didn't want me to feel pressured to stay because of, you know, the uneven power dynamic.

I sat back down, relieved. I didn't want to go either. That's when he blushed and told me he's had a crush on me since our first day. WHAT! WHY? I WORE A BLAZER THE FIRST DAY!

He was torn about what to do because he's technically my boss and didn't want to put me in an uncomfortable position. He seemed genuinely conflicted about it so I did the only thing I could think of to make him feel better: I kissed him. (On the mouth, you dirty bird.)

I think I finally understand the appeal of older men. They actually know what to do with their tongues. (In my mouth! Get your head out of the gutter!) We must have kissed for an hour before saying anything. My face was rubbed raw and surprisingly painful. I asked if he had any face cream, which he also seemed to find charming (thank god).

After applying a healthy dose of Neutrogena Sensitive Skin, we resumed our position on the couch, but this time started talking. About pretty much everything. Maybe not everything, but at least a few important things. I laughed the whole time. Until we fell asleep around 3AM.

I HAVE NEVER BEEN AWAKE UNTIL 3AM. Not in college. Not with Jessie. Not with the flu. I love sleep. But I think I love Ben more.

And before you challenge me: It's not too fast. This could all work out in the end. Our children will be very hairy but cute.

Ava

P.S. I'm totally fucked, right?

Re: HOW DID YOU KNOW?

 Gen Goldman <GEN.GOLDMAN@gmail.com> 9/22/19
to Ava

Oh sweet baby girl. I wish I was there so I could nuzzle you into a bear hug and then hit your head against the wall.

YOU ARE NOT IN LOVE. THIS GUY IS NOT SPECIAL. HE IS NOT THE SOLUTION TO ALL OF YOUR PROBLEMS. HE IS ONLY ATTRACTIVE IN A MAINSTREAM WAY.

I think you already know this, but it sounds like you got played. Hard. You just happened to arrive at his door? He doesn't want to do anything that makes you uncomfortable? He doesn't normally do this??? (I don't know if he actually said that last part, but I'm willing to put someone else's money on it.)

He made you make the first move so he would have plausible deniability. He is a master manipulator who abuses his power to bed interns.

Or he's actually a really nice guy, and you have a special connection.

WHO KNOWS!

P.S. I really don't think it's that second option.

5:24 PM

But you'll admit there is a small chance he's a nice guy and we have a special connection?

No.

But you said . . .

No I didn't.

I have the receipts.

How do I know they're not doctored?

Because I don't know how to use Photoshop!!!

Remember my acne-free summer of 2015?

You should learn how to use Photoshop.

JUST ANOTHER LINK IN THE CHAIN

 Gen Goldman <GEN.GOLDMAN@gmail.com>   9/23/19
to Ava

Here I sit, another beaten-down employee who doesn't even get dental. (Actually maybe I do. I should really check my health plan.)

I've spent the last few hours learning how to code. And by that I mean, looking for college kids who are willing to code for free. All I need is an intern from a wealthy family and this website will be up and running! Maybe I should follow Ben's lead and hire someone I can also sleep with! (I think Coralee might be unemployed . . .)

I'm so bored, Ava. I actually rearranged my three pieces of furniture last night just to pass the time. Turns out they don't match regardless of their placement in my cell/home.

I need a lede. I need a story. I need to have sex.

Is this what it's like to be a loser? How did you survive all these years?

Gen, Official Loser of the Goldman Family (and that's really saying something because my parents are fucked up)

Re: JUST ANOTHER LINK IN THE CHAIN

 Ava Helmer <AVA.HELMER@gmail.com>   9/23/19
to Gen

Hi! I'm sorry for the late reply! Today was the first show of the season and we all went out to celebrate afterward! Halona was actually happy for the first time. It felt like a national holiday so I had a whole glass of cider!

You're not a loser. You're a twenty-two-year-old queer feminazi who is living in rural Florida. I would be more concerned if you were having a *good* time! That place isn't going to open itself up to you like Emerson and Boston. I think if you want to build a life there, you need to go there and do it. Coralee must have at least one educated friend? (WOW I AM CLASSIST WHEN I'M DRUNK! WHO KNEW?! DON'T SAY YOU!)

Maybe we should give you some sort of time limit? Like you plan to stick it out for _____ months and if you still hate it and have nothing to do other than feng shui your studio and abuse interns, you'll leave? That way you're not just a quitter? I can help you look for other jobs in the meantime??? (I hear Asheville, North Carolina is very woke.)

My stomach hurts. How do people consume more than one beverage at a time?

Ben didn't talk to me at all today, but then he held my hand under the table at the bar. It was exhilarating.

I did cry at lunch because he wasn't talking to me. I'm not sure if I'm cut out for this roller coaster of emotions!

AVA HELMER, FEMME FATALE

11:48 PM
I think I'm gonna get a cat.

Tue, Sep 24, 6:23 AM
I found a cat.

7:45 AM
What is going on???
Did you steal a cat?
No!
I'm going to hunt a cat!
Trap.
I'm going to trap a cat.
What is going on?????
I'll tell you later.
I have to pick up a donut.

WOMAN'S BEST FRIEND

 Gen Goldman <GEN.GOLDMAN@gmail.com> 9/24/19
to Ava

I don't know why I didn't think of this before! I'm a single, queer woman from a dysfunctional family! I crave love but I push it away. What will love me unconditionally, but also not that much?

A FUCKING CAT

I spent like three hours last night looking up cats for adoption on Instagram. I flagged a bunch of them, but then fate intervened. Around six this morning, I heard the most horrifying sound of my life. (And I've attended a cappella concerts.) It was a mix between a screech and a moan that was at the highest register a human ear can process.

I immediately assumed alien invasion. (Or horrible neighbor sex.) So I put on a sweatshirt and ventured outside to be teleported somewhere with better city infrastructure. But instead of spotting a UFO, I locked eyes with my soul mate: Tabby. That's right, I'm gonna call her Tabby. Because it's cute and it's too much pressure to think of anything else.

Tabby is a feral feline who is clearly looking for a partner in crime. I tried to approach her, but she's too smart to trust a stranger. After work I'm gonna pick up cat food and milk to leave out on my porch.

She's a wild one alright, but I'm going to tame her.

G

12:32 PM

Couple of questions and concerns.

Shoot.

Cats can't actually drink milk. That's just misinformation from cartoons.

No way!

I'm googling.

12:35 PM

Holy fuck.

I almost killed Tabby!

What do mean you're going to trap her?

She will just be an outdoor cat that you feed?

Where's the love in that?! I'm gonna trap her in a trap and bring her to the vet.

Vets are expensive.

I'm gonna trap her and bring her inside.

She's a wild animal!

No.

She's a cat.

Can't you just sleep with someone inappropriate if you have to act out?

Who says I can't do both!

This cat is going to hurt you.

😎 Like I haven't been hurt before!
🐦 Wow. That's like Ava-level sad.

2:37 PM
🐦 I'm afraid of cats.
😎 I know bb
😎 Tabby is different.
🐦 That's what they all say.

THE HUNGER GAMES

 Ava Helmer <AVA.HELMER@gmail.com>   9/24/19
to Gen

Things have changed. And they've changed fast. It's only day two of tapings and all the interns have turned on each other. You should see the amount of brown nosing. Lacie would win a medal if anyone could get to her through all the shit on her face.

I'm still in shock. Dana complimented Halona's nail beds today. Is it even possible to have a certain kind of nail bed???

Halona announced that at least one intern will be getting a full-time position before the holidays. I think she is trying to instigate psychological warfare for her own enjoyment. I don't even want to work here long term! I want to work in scripted, but now that I *could* potentially work here long term it's all I think about. (Since Halona made the announcement after a very liquid lunch.)

This whole thing makes my (possible) situation with Ben even more complicated. Now he has the power to actually influence my career. If people find out we are involved and then I get the position, it's going to look like I slept my way to the top! (Even though we have yet to have intercourse or even heavy petting.)

Instead of hanging out after the show, everyone went home immediately to "get some rest." Dana is practicing his stand-up in the next room. It is surprisingly misogynistic for a boy named Dana.

Maybe I'm worrying about something that won't even happen since Ben has yet to call or text me. What if I make it to my deathbed, sad and alone, and learn everything could have been different if I was a better kisser???

I'm gonna call my parents.

A

Re: THE HUNGER GAMES

 Gen Goldman <GEN.GOLDMAN@gmail.com>   9/24/19
to Ava

AVA. IF YOU WILL JUST LET ME KISS YOU I CAN ASSURE YOU THAT YOU ARE A GOOD KISSER! UNLESS YOU LET ME KISS YOU I WILL BE UNABLE TO ASSUAGE YOUR FEARS. I'M NOT ASKING FOR ME, I'M BEGGING FOR YOU.

You can't stay on late-night TV. You have too many stories to tell that take longer than an opening monologue.

On a brighter note, Tabby ate the food I put out! Or at least I think it was Tabby. Might have been a raccoon. But, hey, raccoons need to eat too!

Back to my seventh hour of watching *Hannibal* on Amazon. And to think, I used to be somebody. (I am so alone.)

Give your parents a messy kiss for me!

G

Wed, Sep 25, 10:32 AM

I know what I've been doing wrong?

It was just one thing??

Ha. Ha.

- I've been treating my workplace like an office when I should have been treating it like THE OFFICE (2005–2013).
- Not really following.
- PRANKS AVA
- I'M TALKING ABOUT PRANKS
- You shouldn't be!
- This is a real job.
- Not the greatest sitcom of our time.
- Agree to disagree.
- You're such a Toby.
- How dare you!
- I'm Angela.

DWIGHT YOU IGNORANT SLUT

 Gen Goldman <GEN.GOLDMAN@gmail.com>   9/25/19
to Ava

I did it. I cracked these people. After eighteen years of working here (roughly two weeks) I have finally made an impression. (Actually maybe the problem is I made too much of an impression. I always catch Phyllis looking at my nose ring.)

Instead of eating lunch in my car, like I do most days so it looks like I have somewhere to go, I stayed behind and put air horns on everyone's chairs. So when they sat down, the horn blew.

Beau sat down first. HUGE success. His scream was piercing. Floyd followed and almost had a heart attack. I figured everyone would start checking under their chairs, but then I remembered I was in the South. These people don't learn from others' mistakes!

EVERY SINGLE PERSON SAT DOWN (aka Saul and Grady).

By the time Grady collapsed into his leather throne, people were crying from laughing so hard. Myself included.

Looks like I'm not just some techy dyke after all. (No one has said "dyke" with their mouths, but they have said it with their eyes. If they only knew how many dudes have been up in me. Floyd would have an actual heart attack.)

I'm going to put rulers in their desks tomorrow so they can't open their drawers. Turning out to be a VERY productive week!

Gen Halpert

9:43 PM
How do you get away with this stuff???
I have an incredible personality.
And naturally fit body.
You should have been fired.
For a little air horn action???
Please.

🔘 I bet the fastest way for me to get a raise
is to put an alligator in the kitchen.

🔘 DO NOT DO THAT.

🔘 Grady already knows how to wrestle
them. He talks about it all the time.

🔘 I'm afraid of Florida.

🔘 I know bb.

VIP BABY

 Ava Helmer <AVA.HELMER@gmail.com>   9/25/19
to Gen

The craziest thing just happened. Well, the craziest
thing is going to happen. Apparently Halona attended
some benefit last night about the importance of female
leadership and she has decided she needs a mentee
(mostly for appearances). Ben suggested me and now
she wants to take me to lunch tomorrow to "sniff out"
what I'm really made of. WHAT AM I MADE OF?! I'VE
ALWAYS BEEN TOO AFRAID TO KNOW.

I can't stop shaking. Probably because I don't know if
Ben honestly thinks I'll be the best mentee or if he feels
bad for making out with me, or he wants to make out
with me more? (He wants to celebrate tonight at his
place.)

This is crazy. I'm going to go to lunch with Halona
McBride???? What if I get something in my teeth that I
can't get out?? (I'm obviously going to get something in

my teeth, but the real issue is not being able to get it out. Because then I just look like someone who knows she has something in her teeth and doesn't care. Actually . . . maybe that is cool. I should stop buying emergency toothpicks.)

I have so many questions for her! What was *SNL* like?? How does a woman make it in a man's world? Is she really getting a divorce? (God, I hope I don't ask that last one, but I'm afraid it's going to come spilling out of me along with my entire life story.)

WHAT DO I WEAR?!

Maybe I'll ask Ben. He has very good taste. And they seem to have some sort of special relationship, as in, he is the only person I've never seen her yell at.

Is something in the air today? Why are we both having the best day of our professional lives? (Please don't tell me it has to do with "our sign." I'd be more likely to believe magic air.)

None of the other interns know yet. If I end up dead in an alley, question Lacie first.

Ava Helmer
Potential Mentee to the Stars

Re: VIP BABY

 Gen Goldman <GEN.GOLDMAN@gmail.com> 9/25/19
to Ava

Relax! Halona McBride is a person just like anyone else. She farts! She poops! She probably has even had spinach stuck in her perfect veneers. She's going to love you. And if she doesn't then she's just as crazy as she appeared on *Good Morning America.* (I didn't buy that she-took-Ambien-by-accident story for a second!)

Do you remember what her eyes looked like? It was worse than Winona at the SAG Awards! (Free Winona!)

In regards to Benjamin, I'm worried he's going to give you emotional whiplash. Kiss. Ignore. Overwhelm with nice gesture. Sleep with your mom. Profit.

Maybe put off celebrating with him until after your lunch? So he can't take full credit?

TO BE CLEAR: I totally support you using Ben to advance your career. Just make sure you play him before he plays you.

I think I'm gonna text Coralee. I'm on a real high from that air horn prank.

BAH-BAH-BAH-BAAAAAH (air horn noise)

G

9:45 PM
🌑 Don't ask me where I am.
🌑 Okay.

10:14 PM
🌑 I'm at Ben's.
🌑 Duh.

11:57 PM
🌑 I've made a huge mistake.
🌑 I'm trying to do the same.
🌑 But Coralee is real hot and cold.
🌑 She's not hot and cold. She's straight!
🌑 Give your immediate superior a kiss
for me!

**GOOD LUCK ON YOUR FANCY LIFE-CHANGING
LUNCH TODAY!!!**

 Gen Goldman <GEN.GOLDMAN@gmail.com> 9/26/19
to Ava

Also, did you bone Ben?

ENOUGH ABOUT YOU.

As you know, my social life has been nil since I've arrived in swampy, desolate Florida. My deepest relationship has been formed with a feral cat who remains impervious to my charms (and hands). At around 9:30PM, I texted Miss Coralee to ask her to meet me at GOTCHA for a two-for-one whiskey shot evening. (It's not that special. They have that deal every night. I think the whiskey is very watered down.) A half-hour later, she responded, "I'm already here. Where r u?"

This was confusing because she had not confirmed plans at all. So I "scooted my boot" over there fast as I could, only to find her surrounded by a bevy of five o'clock shadows. This was great news because nothing ups my game more than competition.

One of the five o'clock shadows was actually pretty cute but I already had my eye on the little lady. (Turns out, I like guys in cowboy hats, but only when they're not talking.)

I grabbed us four whiskey shots and moseyed my way into the center of the circle, handing two to Coralee who giggled like a schoolgirl. I realized then that she was absolutely sitting on one of their laps. (Bold!) After downing the shots like a champ, I announced I had to pee. Coralee announced she had to pee as well (playing right into my hands). We went to the bathroom together, which is pretty much first base for lesbians.

After we listened to each other pee, she put on waaaaaay too much lip gloss while she told me I should totally wear my hair down sometimes. I would have kissed her right there if I wasn't worried we'd get stuck (it was A LOT of lip gloss).

We spent the rest of the night looking at each other and laughing while the boys tried to impress us. I beat her at pool. She beat me at chugging a beer. I was interested but distant. Like an animal preparing to make its move. (What kind of animal? Should have paid more attention during *Planet Earth*.)

At the end of the night, I walked her home and we stood at her door, sort of lingering. (She lives two blocks from GOTCHA, which actually explains a lot.) She reached forward and I thought she was going to kiss me but then she unbuttoned my top button on my button-down (wow, say *button* again) and said I would look better showing a little skin. She then kissed my cheek and said, "See ya later, sweet pea!"

Her lip gloss is still on my cheek. I think I need to buy better face wash. And a cowboy hat.

What did you end up wearing for your big day? Your clothes from last night? (SEE WHAT I DID THERE??)

Your Sweetest Pea,

Gen

11:37 AM

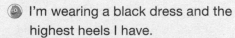 I'm wearing a black dress and the highest heels I have.

So no heels?

There is a wedge.

That's not a heel.

Ben and I didn't have sex.

But he did go down on me.

You're talking to a queer woman.

That's the definition of sex.

Fuck. You're right.

WHY DID I ORDER KALE

 Ava Helmer <AVA.HELMER@gmail.com>   9/26/19
to Gen

I'm honestly not sure where to begin here. You know how there are certain moments and experiences that really stay with you forever? I REALLY hope today was not one of them.

Halona's assistant made us an 11:30 reservation at Gramercy Tavern because the show starts taping at 2:00. I assumed we would go together, but then it was 11:10 and Halona wasn't at the office. So I had to spend $40 on a cab to get there on time and wait for thirty minutes. When Halona walked in the entire atmosphere changed. People started whispering and staring. You could tell she loved it. She kissed a very confused busboy on the cheek, clearly confusing him for the manager.

I had to wave for a full minute before she admitted to herself that I was her lunch date. (Clearly she was hoping for someone more fashionable? Likable? Hotter?) She sat down with a flourish and then launched into one of the most terrifying conversations of my life, which I will now relay to you in screenplay format.

INT. GRAMERCY TAVERN—12:08 PM

HALONA MCBRIDE, 45, eyes her disappointing lunch date across the table. AVA HELMER, an underdeveloped 22, tries to smile even though her mouth is frighteningly dry.

HALONA

Have you been here before?

No time for a response.

HALONA

It's one of my favorites. I love to come here
and think while other people talk at me.
That's the thing no one warns you about.
How much people will talk at you.

Ava says nothing because she doesn't want to "talk at" her.

HALONA

Ben thinks you show real potential. But then
again, you're his type so I have to take it with
a grain of salt.

AVA
(unclear noise)

HALONA
I don't have a lot of time because the show
starts soon and I already ate somewhere
else, but here are quick tips, okay?

AVA
Okay. Thank you. I've always looked up—

HALONA
Tip one. Only suck up to people who want to
be sucked up to. For example, I like it. But
only sometimes. Try to read my mood. How
do you think I'm feeling right now?

Long pause. Ava scrambles for an answer.

HALONA
Good girl. Never tell me how I'm feeling. Tip
two. You will never be good enough,
smart enough, or competent enough to do
what you want to do. You just have to do it
anyway.

Another pause for reaction.

AVA
Wow. That's smart. Thank—

HALONA
Tip three. Every day is a day.

Longest pause so far. Even though the other pauses were uncomfortably long.

> AVA
> Um . . . Is that the whole thing? Every day is
> a day?
>
> HALONA
> Is that not true?
>
> AVA
> No it is . . . I just—
>
> HALONA
> See you at the office, Ava.

And with that she was gone.

If someone told me Halona was a ghost, I would believe them. My skin still has goose bumps. I have never been more afraid in my life.

Re: WHY DID I ORDER KALE

 Gen Goldman <GEN.GOLDMAN@gmail.com> 9/26/19
to Ava

Wow. What a mind fuck. I can't tell if she gave you terrible advice or incredible advice. At least one of the tips seems to just be words that are true? But also, mind blown. Every day IS a day. Wow. Is this my next tattoo?

Were you shocked she knew your name? I kept
expecting her to call you Anna or something.
Sometimes I think people in power do this just to prove
they are in power. I can't wait to be in power.

Do I need to touch on the Ben part of this or can we
both agree he is scum who doesn't deserve you or
your heavily moisturized skin?

5:45 PM

How do we know he is scum??

Uh. . . .

His boss knows his type???

He's clearly done this before.

Or he just has a type! Everyone has a
type!

Yeah, and yours seems to be scumbags

That's not fair!

I like a lot of great guys!

They just don't like me back.

Fair.

I think I'm the only person who doesn't
have a type.

Yes you do!

Unavailable.

We know each other too well.

I prefer anonymity.

Too late! I've seen you poop.

FOR THE LAST TIME THAT IS NOT THE
DEFINITION OF INTIMACY.

It is for me!

9:32 PM

Are you going to tell me what happened with Ben last night?

Because I'm not going to ask.

I'll just make super perverted assumptions.

No! Your imagination is too wild!

I'll email you.

REGARDING THE SCUM

 Ava Helmer <AVA.HELMER@gmail.com>   9/26/19
to Gen

In my defense, if Ben is only pretending to like me he is a good actor. Like good enough to have a sitcom based on his stand-up that isn't canceled after one season. (So Ray Romano not John Mulaney. Even though I love John and would give a non-vital body part away to be with him.)

We went right back to his place after work. I think I was tense or something (I was visibly tense) because he didn't make any sort of move and instead ordered pizza and frozen yogurt. I didn't even know you could order frozen yogurt! New York is the best!

After twenty minutes of scrolling through Netflix, we finally landed on that Leslye Headland movie *Sleeping with Other People*. It was sooooo good. And underrrated. Critics inherently hate rom-coms regardless of quality (a rant for another day).

I kept waiting for him to "make a move" but he didn't. One time I thought he was going to stroke my head but he was just reaching for a glass. (I love it when people stroke my head. It feels better than penetration.)

Around 8:30 I finally caved and kissed him and that's how we got to heterosexual third base. (ORAL.) He went down on me for like forty minutes before I told him I don't know how to orgasm. (MORTIFYING.) He took it really well, once he clarified I had never orgasmed with *anyone* and not just never orgasmed with *him*. He made a sweet joke about enjoying the ride and I giggled. I went to "return the favor" and he said I didn't need to. He was down to just cuddle.

WHAT IS GOING ON! IS THIS A CON! I AM BEING CONNED, RIGHT?

Don't answer that. Ignorance is bliss when it comes to scumbags with great hair.

11:45 PM

🦉 You think he has great hair?

🦉 Weird.

WORK WORK WORK WORK WORK

 Gen Goldman <GEN.GOLDMAN@gmail.com>   9/27/19
to Ava

I've found an intern! His name is Cash (yes, that's his actual name) and he's a student at Jacksonville University majoring in computer science. He is very tall and skinny and wears what I can only assume is the same denim jacket every day. (It's full of holes.) He knows a lot about web design and can help me actually build this website. To be clear, I am not paying him in anything other than life experience and college credit.

I don't want to toot my own horn but I'm going to be an incredible boss. He starts on Monday and I told him it was okay to be late. I can already tell after our brief interview that he sees me as a mentor and confidante. Also, it's very fun to run an interview. Here are some of the best questions I asked him in the parking lot because my desk is too small for two people.

1) Rate how much you respect authority on a 1–5 scale.

2) Rate your emotional intelligence on a 1–5 scale.

3) Who is your favorite Beatle and why? Be careful. There is a wrong answer.

4) What was your first impression of me and how has it changed in the last five minutes?

Really kept him on his toes!

Also, I'm pretty sure Cash is gay but too afraid to come out. So I'll be able to help guide him on that journey as well. Maybe the whole reason I'm in Florida is to help college students explore their sexualities??? If that's not a memoir in the making, I don't know what is!

Gen Goldman,
Cash Something's Boss

3:42 PM

I can't believe they let you have an intern!

They didn't let me. . . .

I found one and then told Grady about it.

And he doesn't care?

Not if he's working for free!

Ah. The American dream.

How many people did you interview?

I already told you.

Cash.

hahahah

Was he the only one who applied?

He was the right fit for the job.

He was also the only one who applied.

Kismet!

Now I can focus on reporting.

I need to go out and be with the people.

Sniff out what they're not telling me.

I've heard Jacksonville has a great zoo if you want to do an article about that.

What is with you and zoos?

I love animals!

I just wish they loved me back . . .

That was one dog, Ava! Get over it!

10:32 PM

I'm making great strides with Tabby.

11:27 PM

That's great!

What are you doing?

Out.

But it's so late!

Who r u

Sat, Sep 28, 1:23 AM

How do people not realize Hannibal is a cannibal????

2:12 AM

They just figured it out.

Way too late.

Everyone is dead.

3:27 AM

- When do you think you'll die?
- My guess is 87 for you.
- 52 for me.
- I should go to bed.

9:42 AM

- Thank you for this disturbing morning reading.
- I am growing increasingly concerned about your mental health and Hannibal obsession.
- THEY'RE ONE AND THE SAME.

A BOY NAMED DANA

 Ava Helmer <AVA.HELMER@gmail.com>   9/28/19
to Gen

I think Dana hates me now. But like in a very passive-aggressive way. I told him all about my lunch with Halona because I *thought* we were friends and roommates who wanted to support each other. . . . He didn't say anything other than "cool." And then asked if I wanted to split an Xbox??? I don't know how to use an Xbox but I said sure because I suddenly felt very worried about the state of our relationship. So now I'm out $150 and I'll probably have to find a new roommate.

I don't get it. It's not like the lunch went well and I'm suddenly Halona's golden child. If that was the case, I would understand the weirdness/jealousy (and it wouldn't even bother me because I'd be Halona's golden child). But this feels petty. And mean. Maybe he knows about Ben? Should I tell him about Ben? What is going on with Ben?

Having Dana give me the cold shoulder makes me realize how much I depend on him. I don't really have any friends here other than the other interns. And if they turn on me, I might have to reach out to Grabby Igor who is working in finance somewhere downtown. (I ran into him this summer. He's actually not grabby anymore but it's too good a nickname to let go. I assume that's why everyone called me Anxious Ava for so long. Even though that's not nearly as clever.)

UGGGGHHHHH

Why can't things be easy???

Anxious Ava

2:35 PM

I hate to break this to you but your life IS easy.

????

You're working an unpaid internship in the best city while your parents support your pizza habit.

Well when you put it that way!

I sound like a spoiled brat!

Who is also sleeping with her boss.

I need to find a therapist ASAP.

I can't believe I agreed to the Xbox.

SECRET UNDERBELLY OF FERNANDINA BEACH

Gen Goldman <GEN.GOLDMAN@gmail.com> 9/29/19

to Ava

Last night I went out on the town to buy a pint of ice cream and wallow in my celibacy. It was supposed to be a real quick in and out job. 7-Eleven accepts Apple Pay so I didn't even need my wallet. But then my bleeding heart led me astray. And by that I mean I started talking to a homeless person. The following is a recorded interview, on the record, from Lyle Rainbow, 24(?), about his life on the streets as a gay man.

Lyle: Can I get something to eat?
Reporter: I don't have my wallet.
Lyle: How are you going to buy anything?

(pause)

Reporter: What do you want?
Lyle: One of those hot dogs and some chips.
Reporter: You got it!

(Reporter returns with food.)

Lyle: Aw, sweet! Ice cream.
Reporter: No, that is for me.
Lyle: That's fine. It's not like I have a freezer.

(Starts to rain.)

Lyle: Fuck.
Reporter: Are you going to go to a shelter?
Lyle: *(snorting)* I can't.
Reporter: Why?

Asking "why?" is the simplest tool in a reporter's tool kit. A "why?" can unlock kingdoms, break barriers, overthrow tyrants. The best thing you can do as a journalist is keep asking people "why?" Please note, this can also backfire and cause you to lose the story. Use "why?" wisely.

Luckily, this time, it did NOT backfire. And instead, opened a floodgate of homophobia, hypocrisy and discrimination. Apparently the largest (and only) homeless shelter in the area does not allow LGBTQ occupants unless they are participating in conversion therapy. (Not so) big reveal: it's run by a church. Apparently Open All Doors congregation has a strict close-some-doors policy.

I AM GOING TO BURN THIS PLACE TO THE GROUND! Or at least publicly shame them into changing their policy. I'm going to talk to Grady about this first thing in the morning and if he doesn't let me pursue it I'm quitting.

Okay, I have to run. Lyle wants breakfast.

THIS DAY WE FIGHT!

(That's from *The Lord of Rings*. I wanted to save you the google.)

G

10:43 AM

What do you mean "Lyle wants breakfast"???

Did you let a homeless man sleep in your studio apartment??

I think you're getting the wrong impression of Lyle.

He's very cool.

Why is he homeless?

Drugs. And his parents won't help him because of the gay thing.

What kind of drugs????

Purple Drank.

That's a bad one!

I was kidding. I didn't ask. But he's clean now I think. He just has nowhere to go.

Because of the fucking do-good Christians and their hypocrisy.

I'm very proud of you for standing up for a just cause, but I also think you should ask him to leave and change your locks.

JUST TO BE SAFE

No one is safe in this economy.

I'll have Open All Doors pray for you.

DOUBLE LIFE

 Ava Helmer <AVA.HELMER@gmail.com>   9/29/19
to Gen

Just got back from dinner with my secret boyfriend. That's right. Ben is officially my boyfriend. I'm just not allowed to tell anyone.

I know what you're thinking. Why does it need to be a secret? Is he ashamed of me? Is he secretly married? Has my chemical imbalance shifted into schizophrenia and he's a figment of my imagination?

I thought all of that too. But Ben provided me with a much better reason: office politics. If the other interns find out I'm dating the (adorable) boss, I'll have a target on my back. Plus it's technically against the rules. And you know how much I hate breaking the rules! So we've agreed to keep it on the hush-hush until my internship is over. And if I somehow end up being full-time we will deal with it then.

How did all of this happen? Thanks for asking! I was bumming around my apartment, looking for therapists in-network, when Ben called and told me to come to a bar a few blocks from my apartment for trivia night with his friends. That's right! I met his friends. Or at least three of them!

This was a very high-stakes event for me because I am horrible at trivia but I am even worse at losing. I kept having to tell myself that I still have value even though I don't seem able to recall any American history. (This might be for the best because America has done some fucked-up stuff!)

Ben crushed trivia by the way. I've never been more "turnt up." (Is that the right expression? Please advise.) He knew everything! Sports! Music! Movies! Sports! I was enamored. And so was the waitress. But he mostly ignored her BECAUSE I'M HIS GIRLFRIEND.

Wow. I have never had to keep a secret before. Or I have, but I have failed to keep it. It's burning a hole inside of my esophagus (or maybe that was the turkey chili). HOW AM I SUPPOSED TO STAY CALM? I'M JUST SUPPOSED TO GO INTO WORK TOMORROW AND NOT ANNOUNCE I'M IN A COMMITTED RELATIONSHIP WITH SOMEONE OVER 5'10"???

I am not strong enough. This is never going to work.

Is that homeless man still sleeping in your apartment?

A

11:23 PM

🦉 Ava.

🦉 Yes?

🦉 Do you think "turnt" means turned on?

11:34 PM

🦉 Ava.

🦉 Answer the question.

🦉 LEAVE ME ALONE

🦉 hahahahahahahaha

🦉 Brb while I group email our entire high
school.

🦉 Like you still have their contact info.

🦉 Shit.

TAKING THEM DOWN FROM THE INSIDE

 Gen Goldman <GEN.GOLDMAN@gmail.com> 9/30/19
to Ava

Today I prepared for battle. I wore my most "sensible/
straight" outfit and bought half a dozen jelly donuts. I
brushed my hair and thought of nice things to say
about fishing. ("Oh, wow! You really caught that fish
with a hook!") I was prepared to be shot down and I
was prepared to fight anyway. I even kicked in Grady's
door with my foot to prove I was serious.

Things did not go as planned. Instead of confronting a 250-pound mound of skepticism and disinterest, Grady immediately took to my story and urged me to investigate further. I think it helps that Open All Doors is a Methodist congregation and Grady is a "loosely" practicing Presbyterian. (Apparently Methodists are backwards and Presbyterians have much bigger hearts. Who knew! I thought they were all bad!)

He wants a more official interview from Lyle Rainbow and any of his persecuted friends. He also wanted me to speak with the head of the shelter but I offered him one better. I proposed going undercover as a gay woman with nowhere to go (which is eerily close to the truth). I'd secretly record the interaction and expose them for the haters they truly are. (The official policy is "a warm bed for anyone who needs to lay their head." Yeah, right.)

I can't believe he's on board. Things are really turning around in the swamp.

How's Day 1 of your double life? Have you blown the whole thing yet? I'm assuming even the security guard knows by now.

G

Re: TAKING THEM DOWN FROM THE INSIDE

 Ava Helmer <AVA.HELMER@gmail.com>   9/30/19
to Gen

Go Grady! Go Grady! Go Grady!

This is such great news! Who knew bringing down the
Methodists would be Grady's holy grail! You should
pretend everything you're investigating has to do with
the Methodists from now on!

When are you going to go undercover? What are you
going to wear? Please don't use this as an excuse to
not shower. I hope you still shower!

It's almost lunchtime and I have yet to spill the beans.
Things are slightly better with me and Dana so I really
don't want to jeopardize that. Full disclosure: I have
been bribing him with pastries.

Ben is doing that "ignoring me thing" again but this time
I don't care because we've defined the relationship as
in we have an actual relationship. My parents are
coming to visit in like two weeks. Do you think he will
want to meet them? Or will that be too soon? It's really
important to me that he meets them. Why? Probably
something to do with the media? (I like to blame all
my problems on "the media." It's extra biting because
as an intern for *Mind the Gap with Halona McBride* I
am officially part of the problem. Which is the media. If
that wasn't clear.)

Okay, I'm spazzing out. Halona is on a rampage this morning so everyone is on edge. She claims to be mad about gun control but everyone thinks she's just hungover from a late night with her new illicit lover. (The rumor mill is out of control over here. Apparently some girl in accounting is the bastard daughter of Bill Gates? Although I think she might have started that one for attention. It's pretty boring over in accounting.)

In brighter news, there's going to be an on-air segment featuring an intern in tomorrow's show. A really quick on and off spot. But now everyone is freaking out and submitting their acting reels to Ben. (Why do they all have acting reels? Unclear.) I told Ben not to consider me because I don't want to get any special treatment. He said I was underqualified anyway. (He was joking. I think.)

It's actually a relief that I have no interest in performing. It's one less thing to fail at!

Oh! I've been meaning to ask you! Do I need to learn to cook or can I just get by without knowing how for the rest of my life?

I eagerly await your enlightened opinion.

A

4:32 PM

- You don't need to know how to cook.
- But you should learn how to survive a zombie apocalypse.
- Yeah right.
- Why would I want to survive that?
- Sounds awful.
- Fine. At least learn how to heat up ramen.
- On it!

SPEAKING OF ACTING . . .

 Gen Goldman <GEN.GOLDMAN@gmail.com>   10/1/19
to Ava

Ever heard of "going method?" Because my girl Coralee sure has!

Let me rewind a bit. After work last night, I asked Coralee if she wanted to help me out with an assignment. She never responded. Around 9:30, she showed up at my house. I'm starting to think this girl treats her phone like a pager. It's adorably infuriating. Luckily I was wearing my best pajamas: tiny shorts with cowboys on them. I have no idea how they came to be in my possession, but they fit great.

I think she was already a bit tipsy so I offered her more wine because that's what good hosts do. I explained the shelter situation and asked if she would be willing to pose as my girlfriend. Undercover. For the story.

"What'll I have to do, darling?" she murmured into my ear. (Not really, but she murmurs all the time. It can be hard to hear her.) I explained we would have to hold hands and ask to share a bed. It probably wouldn't go further than that before they asked us to leave.

She nodded so slowly I thought maybe she'd fallen asleep. But she was wide awake, baby! Her main concern was us not passing for a couple since we've never slept together. Apparently, people change once they've slept together and everyone can tell. Change how? The way they touch each other. The way they look at each other . . .

This was one of those moments when I thanked the spirits for not having a penis because I would definitely be the mayor of boner city! Vaginas are so much more discreet.

I couldn't totally tell if she was telling me this because she wanted to sleep together or this was just some hillbilly mysticism. I didn't want to press my luck so I suggested a compromise. What if we just kissed, so people could tell we'd at least been physical?

She giggled and acted shocked.

Coralee: "I've never kissed a girl before."
Reporter: "Never?"
Coralee: "Well, never in *private.*"

And with that, ladies and gentlemen and everyone in between, I was in! WE MADE OUT! For like two hours. (Okay, maybe it was like twenty minutes but it felt like a lifetime.) Her lips are so soft without that awful lip gloss. I asked for her secret. And she told me it was lard. She uses lard. Try not to think about it too much. I'm doing my best not to.

We're going to go to the shelter tomorrow night after I talk to a few of Lyle's buddies during the day. I'd say wish me luck, but I think that's what the lard is for????

G

Re: SPEAKING OF ACTING . . .

 Ava Helmer <AVA.HELMER@gmail.com>   10/1/19
to Gen

Couple of very important things:

1) NEVER talk to me about lard. The only way that I am able to make it in this cruel, cruel world is a complete denial of how processed foods are made. I also block out everything regarding dust. Because it is human skin. And I CAN'T know that. What were we talking about? I've already forgotten.

2) Am I literally the only person on the planet who can resist your pheromones? I'm obviously obsessed with

your mind, but no part of me wants anything to do with your tongue. I've seen your toothbrushes. They're barely used. I just shuddered thinking about your coffee breath . . .

3) I can't believe you get to go undercover! That is so fun! Can I buy your life rights for one dollar if this thing really blows up? I've never thought of myself as a biopic kind of girl, but last night I stayed up until 12:30 on a weeknight so really anything is possible!

Please keep me updated!! Especially regarding Coralee. As we both know a lot more girls are willing to tongue a mouth than a vagina. And you deserve a tongue in your vagina!

LOVE YOU!

A

3:45 PM

I feel like we are both secret agents.

Tell me more . . .

You're going on a spy mission later and I have to pretend not to be in love with my immediate superior.

I don't know how you do it.

I have a couple hives.

Adds up.

Might just be the cold.

I can't believe so many people choose to live in the cold.

It's not always a choice.

EXPOSED

 Gen Goldman <GEN.GOLDMAN@gmail.com>   10/2/19
to Ava

FERNANDINA BEACH, FLA.—Open All Doors Homeless Shelter has long been hailed as a haven for the county's growing homeless population. But despite its name, Open All Doors has a closed-door policy against the already disenfranchised LGBTQ community. Cub reporter Genevieve Goldman went undercover to see exactly what happens when you ask for help but don't fit the "community guidelines."

Late Tuesday evening, Ms. Goldman arrived at the shelter with a female companion. (Many bystanders reported they looked really good together.) Ms. Goldman approached the front desk and inquired about a bunk for the evening. Sister Thompson, a volunteer, said they had two beds available as long as they had IDs and were willing to hand over all potential weapons. Ms. Goldman thanked the elderly nun and said two beds wouldn't be necessary. She and her girlfriend could easily sleep in one so as not to take up much-needed resources.

It was at this time that Sister Thompson assessed Ms. Goldman and her curvy companion with new eyes, bristling at the sight before her. Lesbians! Good god! With a new attitude, the nun informed the aforementioned couple that Open All Doors has a strict morality clause for those staying in their shelter. While Jesus forgives us for our sins (thank you, Jesus), the shelter will not support continued homosexuality. If Ms. Goldman and her "friend" want to stay at Open All Doors they must cease physical contact and attend "reparative therapy" before partaking in free services.

Ms. Goldman inquired for further information regarding reparative therapy. Sister Thompson was delighted at her interest and told her Reverend Ford would be holding a session in the common room before dinner if they would like to attend.

And attend they did! For over an hour, Reverend Ford advised the couple to resist the urge of forbidden sex and instead turn those desires into more productive endeavors. Such as gardening. Ms. Goldman took this opportunity to ask, "Why gardening?" The reverend explained that we are all put on this earth to procreate in some way. If it is not by bearing a child, one can "give birth" to other types of life. Also, the shelter has a new garden.

At this moment, Ms. Coralee found herself unable to stifle her laughter and caused a disturbance. The reverend confronted her and instead of cowing to his wishes, she kissed Ms. Goldman right on the mouth and screamed, "Love wins!" Both women were quickly escorted out. Fortunately, Ms. Goldman had been recording the entire exchange.

Love does win.

This has been Genevieve Goldman of *The Fernandina Beach Centennial.*

Check out our new website coming soon courtesy of unpaid labor.

Re: EXPOSED

 Ava Helmer <AVA.HELMER@gmail.com>   10/2/19
to Gen

SLOW CLAP! Amazing work. When will you get to write about it? Was Grady impressed? Are you in love with Coralee? Can I get a free subscription to the new website through nepotism?

I, too, have had an exciting twenty-four hours. One of our segment producers has menstrual cramps and the first-aid kit was out of Midol so I got to go to Duane Reade and save the day. I can feel my brain deteriorating. I need to start writing at night. Or on the weekends. I'd ask you to hold me accountable but we both know that's a waste of time. (Remember when we went on a diet together and you tried to ruin mine so you could eat cheese again?)

What should I write about?!!

A

7:25 PM

Political thriller.

Ooo! About what?

A former soldier who has been brainwashed by the communists gets elected president.

That's The Manchurian Candidate.

Twist! The president is a woman.

No one will believe that!

You're right. I'll keep thinking.

8:47 PM

I think your dad is really funny.

. . .

Maybe write a movie about him!

What about him?

I CAN'T DO EVERYTHING FOR YOU!

11:29 PM

OK! I got it!

What?

11:58 PM
 Fuck. I forgot.

THE DOCTOR WILL SEE ME NOW

Ava Helmer <AVA.HELMER@gmail.com>   10/3/19
to Gen

I just got back from seeing my new therapist, Dr. Grimm, Ph.D. Dr. Grimm is surprisingly upbeat! I think it must be her married name. She's pretty young. Or maybe she just has great skin. I wonder if she worries about losing her good skin. I know I do! It feels like only a matter of time before I wake up and see my mother's face staring back at me. Maybe it will be nice. I do miss her!

For the first time maybe ever I did a weird thing. I didn't lie exactly, but I did omit. Pretty much everything about Ben. It's not like we had time to talk about him (there was a lifetime of mental illness to catch up on) but when she asked if I was seeing anyone I sort of evaded the question? Now I feel guilty. It's one thing to lie to myself, but I really shouldn't lie to my therapist!

I'll just make sure I tell her next week. It'll be the first thing out of my mouth! Unless it's really cold again and then I'll have to ask her to turn up the heat.

DON'T YELL AT ME!!

A

Re: THE DOCTOR WILL SEE ME NOW

 Gen Goldman <GEN.GOLDMAN@gmail.com> 10/3/19
to Ava

I'm not yelling at you, but don't you think this is a bad sign? Maybe you know on some level this isn't a healthy relationship? And that's coming from me . . . the queen of unhealthy relationships.

8:13 PM

Ben just cooked me dinner.

Isn't that the definition of healthy?

Depends on what he made.

It doesn't matter what he made! He made it for me!

Mac and cheese?

ARE YOU INSIDE HIS APARTMENT?

GREETINGS FROM DOWN UNDER

 Gen Goldman <GEN.GOLDMAN@gmail.com>   10/5/19

to Ava

Psych! I'm still in Florida. Which technically is down from you if you consider South down. Nothing is technically down when you think about the planet as a rotating globe in the galaxy . . . But I'm getting ahead of myself! (JK I have nothing else to say about the galaxy . . . FOR NOW!)

I spent all day yesterday working on my story. Grady even sat with me during the afternoon to make sure it reads well and doesn't appear too biased. (Since Open All Doors is technically a private organization it doesn't *have* to accept LGBTQ patrons. We're trying to nail them on the false-advertising, conversion-therapy angle.) The first story is going to run Monday and if it gets any traction Grady wants me to do a profile on Lyle Rainbow and one or two of his friends.

Beau is worried we will lose local advertisers but Grady thinks it's worth it. No one remembers the paper exists so it can't hurt to stir up a little controversy. Did I tell you I caught Grady reading Dale Carnegie's book *How to Win Friends & Influence People*? I think he is really ready to shake things up! I want him to read *Lean In* but I don't want to rush his transformation into an actual person.

Coralee kept texting me but I was so busy I couldn't write back. It wasn't even intentional but now she's hooked and wants to hang out later. I'm like the human opposite of conversion therapy.

HOW ARE YOU????

4:35 PM

Excuse my language but FUCK ME IN THE ASS

Okay. Be there in about four hours.

I think Dana knows about me and Ben.

Shit!

So you don't want me to fuck you in the ass?

Gen! Focus!

Sorry. Sorry.

What happened???

Dana and I were assembling a new coffee table together and he was reading the instructions on my phone when Ben texted me.

BABY GIRL! NEVER LET ANYONE USE YOUR PHONE WHEN YOU'RE HAVING AN ILLICIT AFFAIR!

I've never had one before!

I'm a rookie!

What did the text say?

Nothing crazy but it's weird for our boss to be texting me on the weekend unless . . .

You're banging him!

Did Dana confront you about it?

No.

He just said, "Ben texted you." And handed me back my phone.

Ouch.

That's ROUGH.

I KNOW!

SEND HELP!

I don't know any cis straight men! They're a mystery to me!

Your boss is a CSM. Your dad . . .

Oh, right.

4:52 PM

I guess you can talk to him about it???

It took you twenty minutes for that???

Men are scary! Aren't you following the news???

BRB while I go ruin the one true friendship I have in a five-hundred-mile radius.

Oh, do you know someone in North Carolina?

4:59 PM

No response??

I had to google that!

WELL THAT WENT WELL

Ava Helmer <AVA.HELMER@gmail.com>   10/5/19
to Gen

NOT!

Per your suggestion, and the suggestion of pretty much every advice column I spent one hour scouring, the best way to communicate with a roommate or friend is DIRECTLY! Who knew! Leaving passive-aggressive notes on the fridge is heavily frowned upon in the mature community.

SO! I took a gulp of orange juice (I'm trying to get off juice but desperate times . . .) and I knocked on Dana's closed door. He invited me in and suddenly I was inside the one part of the apartment I rarely frequent because why would I? It smells like a litter box. (And no, we do not have a cat.)

Normally when I knock on Dana's door, he hops up and we go into the living room, but tonight he stayed put, forcing me to sit on his "vintage" (used) desk chair. I made sure my hair didn't touch it. The following conversation is based on true events but might not be entirely accurate due to the recounter's fragile state of mind and recent lack of antioxidants. (Blueberries are fucking expensive!)

Young Woman: Hey.
Young Man: What's up?
Young Woman: I wanted to talk about earlier.

No response. A clear FUCK YOU.
Young Woman: You're probably wondering why Ben is texting me on a weekend.
Young Man: Nope.
Young Woman, *visibly thrown*: You're not wondering?
Young Man: Nope. I know why he's texting you. You guys are hooking up.
BEAT
Young Woman: Yeah . . .
Young Man: I just hope you're careful. He's a bit of a sleazeball from what I've heard.
Young Woman: What do you mean?
Young Man: Jenna told me he bangs a lot of interns.
Young Woman: Why would Jenna say that?!
Young Man: I don't know. Because it's true.
Young Woman: Really? Because he told me he *never* does this.
Young Man snorts.
Young Man: It's not my business. Just be careful. . . . Are you okay? . . . Hey, don't cry. . . . Come on. Maybe it's just a rumor!
Young Woman: Do you think so?!
Young Man: No.

The rest of the conversation dissolved into snot and whining so I'll spare you from it. I know Dana wishes he could have been spared from it . . .

ANYWAY, my life is falling apart and I'm a cliche wrapped inside a stereotype.

Ava

Re: WELL THAT WENT WELL

 Gen Goldman <GEN.GOLDMAN@gmail.com>   10/6/19
to Ava

Regarding Ben's philandering and classic male sense of entitlement: fuck that guy. I hate him and he never deserved you!

Also, who is Jenna? That married lesbian Dana has a crush on? If so, married lesbians are the best sources regarding straight douchebags since they have no skin in the game. We should trust her with our lives.

I'm sorry, boo. But it's good to know the truth now and not in five months when you've put a deposit down on a wedding venue. (Five months was not a typo. I know how your brain works.)

What are you going to do? Confront him? Ghost him? Hit him? Hire someone else to hit him?

I support all four options, but think the last one makes the most sense.

I'm here if you need me! No plans for the day other than trapping and seducing a feral cat! Ah! Youth!

Gen

11:37 AM

The one good thing about having my heart ripped out of my chest is free muffins.

Dana bought me a muffin.

What kind?

Some sort of bran.

Gross.

I mean . . . GREAT!

Good for fiber!

How are you doing?

Bad.

He keeps texting me.

Are you replying?

Yes . . .

AVA!

GEN!

I don't know how I want to play this yet. So I'm pretending everything is okay.

Although I'm using wayyyyy less exclamation points than usual.

So just the regular amount?

😊

Maybe you should make out with Dana just for fun.

Yeah right. I'm completely straight. And we both know he only likes lesbians.

My kinda guy.

TARGET APPREHENDED

 Gen Goldman <GEN.GOLDMAN@gmail.com> 10/6/19
to Ava

I am now the proud owner of a feral animal. That's right, Tabby is in my apartment as we speak, clawing at my bathroom door, trying to escape. Just how I like my guests!

How did I catch her, you ask? Good old-fashioned bribery. I went and bought a large filet of salmon and put it right inside my door. Then I went and hid so she wouldn't see me. About twenty minutes into crouching, Tabby finally gave in to her gluttony and came inside. I jumped up and shut the door. She did NOT like that but I have put vodka on all of my scratches so I'm sure I'm fine. (Why would anyone buy Neosporin when they can just use vodka? Should I start a lifestyle blog?)

I managed to kick the salmon into the bathroom and now she's trapped! She has no choice but to love and fear me. Is this how most of your relationships start?

I'm going to try to get her to a vet if she ever calms down. I'm hoping they'll cover the charges since I have saved an innocent feline from a life on the streets!

My arm is bleeding again.

LOVE YOU!

G

4:21 PM

Gen!

You have to go to a doctor!

?

Feral cats are full of diseases.
ESPECIALLY if they scratch you.

Says who?

Common sense!

And 5/5 doctors!

I think I'm fine.

The skin isn't that raised. It's just
bubbling.

GEN!

Don't worry! I cut my arm off already so
it won't spread.

STOP THIS

Meow!

Oh no! I turned into a rabid cat!

Meow!

I don't think cats can have rabies. That's
just dogs and raccoons.

Why do you know so much about
cats???

Just go to a doctor okay?

Fine. But it'll cost you.

Happy to pay!

9:12 PM

Hello, Ava.

Hello . . .

I've heard a lot about you.

Who is this?

You know who this is.

Oh no.

Tabby?

🐱

What did you do to Gen?

Don't worry about it.

She's just one big hairball now.

That's disgusting, Tabby.

Meow.

Mon, Oct 7, 6:45 AM

Please be awake.

I'm freaking out.

I have to see Ben.

He was gone all weekend and now I have to see him and I want to throw up.

Is this why you're not supposed to date coworkers?

WAKE UP, TABBY!

8:12 AM

I'm awake!!

Am I too late?!

Have you self-destructed?

9:03 AM

Still alive.

Barely.

What happened??

Too crazy right now. Will write later.

Okay.

So far none of my coworkers have realized I'm now possessed by a cat.

So much for sniffing out a good story!

DON'T YELL AT ME

 Ava Helmer <AVA.HELMER@gmail.com>   10/7/19
to Gen

Ben and I are still together, okay? I'm not proud. I'm not happy. I'm full of shame.

At the same time, I think this is the right decision. At least for now. Please bear with me for my opening argument:

Ladies and gentlemen of the jury: the day started out like any other. Ava Helmer arrived at work fifteen minutes before everyone else due to a chemical imbalance in her brain. She spent the time wiping down her desk area and contemplating a life of loneliness. Perhaps she would get a dog? Or a friendly hedgehog. Right in the middle of a quill-filled daydream, Ava's direct superior and current lover, Ben, entered from behind. To clarify, he did not enter *her* from behind. He entered the *room* from behind, causing her to shriek with alarm.

After a brief laugh, Ava turned her back on him, ostensibly to return to work (although as an unpaid intern, she had very little work to do), but he immediately caught on to her ragged disposition. He demanded to know the source of her "bad attitude" and "bitchiness." To clarify, *she* was not a bitch. Her *actions* were bitchy. Both Ava and Ben confirm the latter to be true.

Ava proceeded to inform Ben about her conversation with Mr. Dana and the accusations regarding Ben's past behavior. Ben did not seem at all surprised by the allegations and remained calm and collected. He conceded two past relationships with subordinates but said they were purely sexual in nature and did not hold the emotional weight of his current engagement. He urged Ava not to engage in office gossip. That was one of the main reasons they had decided not to tell anyone of their relationship. Ava apologized and relayed the series of unfortunate events that caused Dana to find out about the affair. Ben forgave her right before the two were interrupted by other colleagues demanding a coffee run.

In conclusion, Ava is a pussy. But she is a pussy in love. She not so eagerly awaits the verdict.

I rest my case,

Ava Helmer, Esq.

5:13 PM

Never waste your money on law school.

Why not? Because I'm innately talented at it?

No.

Opposite.

How did this conversation end with YOU apologizing to HIM?

I said I wouldn't tell anyone and now Dana knows . . .

Who gives a fuck!

He should be begging for your forgiveness, not manipulating himself into the role of the victim.

Do you want to go to law school?

No.

They can't handle my truth!

Finally a reference I understand!

He's gaslighting you, Ava.

Full disclosure.

I have never totally understood that term.

manipulate (someone) by psychological means into questioning their own sanity.- MW

Oh I don't think he did that.

I've never presumed to be sane.

YOU'RE MISSING THE POINT

I know. It's called deflecting.

Speaking of, how's your undercover story?

IT'S GOING REALLY WELL SO STOP ASKING

I have to go. I love you!

Where?

Where??????????????
I'm gonna send Tabby to find you.

11:35 PM

I'm very disappointed in you.
Sssh. I'm trying to sleep.
Where????

SINCE YOU ASKED . . .

 Gen Goldman <GEN.GOLDMAN@gmail.com>   10/8/19
to Ava

Here is a link to the story: www.fbcennential.com/open
-all-doors-homophobia

It also ran in print today but it looks better on the
website because Cash actually knows what he's doing!
So far there are five comments, mostly about my
author photo. I'm gonna try to get it picked up by bigger
LGBT outlets. . . .

I asked Open All Doors for a response but they didn't
want to give one, which is great. I love a "no comment."
Makes them seem guilty AF. I'm interviewing Lyle
Rainbow tomorrow for his profile. In the meantime I'll
be sending flirty texts to Coralee and wondering when
this schmuck in N.Y. is going to break my best friend's

heart. My guess is next Thursday. Wanna put money on it?

In brighter news, Tabby has significantly warmed up to me and didn't make a break for it when I opened the door this morning. She either feels at home or has given up completely. Either way, I'll take it! I have an appointment with a low-cost vet later today. Going to have to try to catch her in a trash bag since those carrier things are mad expensive. Gonna try to make Coralee come with me since she has a paw tattoo on her wrist so she must be some kind of animal lover.

Kittens and hoes,

GEN

2:32 PM

You're joking about the trash bag right?

Gen, you can't put a cat in a trash bag.

6:12 PM

Wow. You were right about the trash bag thing.

If Tabby has a disease, I now definitely have it too.

Good thing I always steal Band-Aids!

7:07 PM

Turns out, I do NOT have what Tabby is carrying.

Because it's roughly 3 to 5 kittens.

She's pregnant?????

Big time!

I'm gonna be a grandma!

Hate to be the voice of reason here but . . . Is it too late to abort?

Ava! This is my legacy we're talking about!

Who else is going to carry on the family name?

I'm gonna name them all Gen.

I can't believe for a brief moment in time, I was the irresponsible one.

Hey! I didn't get knocked up! Tabby did.

And it's not like she's still dating the guy.

I don't tolerate emotional abuse in my home.

Had enough of that my entire childhood.

Yeah. Your home life was v sad.

I strive to do better for my children!

8:32 PM

I forgot to congratulate you on the article!!

It was great!

Hey, thanks!

But it's all about the children now.

Oy vey.

VIRAL (IN THE GOOD WAY)

 Gen Goldman <GEN.GOLDMAN@gmail.com> 10/9/19

to Ava

The article is a hit! Multiple media outlets have reposted or quoted it. It's officially the highlight of my professional career. I'm clearly flourishing in my isolation. Florida is my new natural habitat. Humidity is cleansing! The constant threat of a gator attack is thrilling! Our governor is probably only homophobic as a bit! (That last one is probably too optimistic.)

Grady says I can put a rush on my profile of Lyle Rainbow for publication on Friday. I'm gonna meet with him tonight on the beach. He camps out there with friends. Grady asked if I wanted Beau to accompany me for "protection" but I think most people want to fight Beau so it wouldn't be a good idea. I am going to bring Tabby if I can get her into this harness I bought. It's not good to leave a pregnant woman alone.

What if I somehow bring down the entire Christian institution? That would be a great legacy. Probably the highest of honors since saints won't exist anymore . . .

How is your HUMP DAY treating you?

G

Re: VIRAL (IN THE GOOD WAY)

 Ava Helmer <AVA.HELMER@gmail.com>   10/9/19
to Gen

Oh my god!! This is huge!! I just saw someone from USC share the link on FB. She doesn't even know I know you! Am I famous now? Wow! This is such a rush! No wonder people want to be successful!

Speaking of famous, successful people . . . Halona took up meditation over the weekend and has completely transformed. (If you believe anything that comes out of her mouth.) I saw her sitting cross-legged in her office a few minutes ago with her eyes open but rolled back? Looked a lot more like she was possessed than enlightened but what do I know! I'm actively lying to my mental health professional!

In case you haven't been keeping vigilant track of my social calendar, my parents are coming this weekend. Ben wants to meet them. And I'm not just projecting that desire because I want it to be true. He's the one who brought it up! He thinks we should all grab dinner Friday and see a matinee on Sunday. I am very excited. So excited that I won't even listen when you tell me this is a bad idea.

Here's why I won't listen:

1) I'm trying to "live in the moment" and "embrace happiness" before we all inevitably die. Potentially in a nuclear fallout.

2) My parents are happy someone (anyone) is spending time with me. Will they *like* Ben? Of course not. He's old and my boss and also a bit arrogant if we're being honest. But he is alive and no one is paying him to stick around.

3) What is the point of your twenties if not to make mistakes? Seriously. I'm asking. If you can provide me with other points, maybe I will change my behavior because right now all I'm doing is getting coffee and forming short-term relationships.

4) I've never done drugs. (So I'm allowed to do this, right?)

Maybe I should take a page from Halona's pamphlet and try meditating. JK, my mind is too wild to tame! I wish I could get these thoughts on lock! (This is my first time using the term "on lock." Does it work for me? I almost deleted it.)

Anyway, I'm very excited to see my parents and have them ask all about you like they always do. I'm sure my mom will text you about the article if she hasn't already. She spends way too much time on social media.

LOVE YOU PROUD OF YOU WANT TO KISS YOU,

A

4:52 PM

GUESS WHO JUST TEXTED ME

Called it!

What?

I told you my mom would text you!

OHHH

Yeah. She did.

But guess who ELSE texted me.

The one and only D.C. wunderkind Alex Cassidy. [YouTube link to the music video for "Return of the Mack"]

Alex Cassidy of Alex and Gen??

One and the same. Although based on how little we talk it sounds like he's rebranded.

What did he say???

He sent me a link TO MY OWN ARTICLE and wrote "congrats."

Like does he think I don't know about my own article???

Why did he send me the link??????

Who knows! He behaves in strange and mysterious ways!

There's also the chance that he still doesn't know how the internet works.

Ugh.

He's like a 45-year-old grandpa.

I miss him.

What are you going to write back?

I'll let you know. Probably won't respond for a few days.

OH HOW I'VE MISSED THESE GAMES

You know he isn't actually playing games with you, right?

Who cares as long as I win!

HANGING WITH THE HOMIES

 Gen Goldman <GEN.GOLDMAN@gmail.com> 10/10/19
to Ava

Next time we are together we have to rewatch *Clueless.* ICONIC.

Putting my profile of Lyle together right now. You're never going to believe this but his real name isn't LYLE RAINBOW. His given name is Mike Scanlon and he's from Minnesota. He renamed himself after his parents threw him out. He found his way to Florida since he loves warm weather and thought people on the coasts would be more accepting. (I think he forgot Florida is a red state.)

The most fucked-up thing is that he actually started working for Open All Doors as a youth ambassador until they found out he was gay and kicked him to the curb like day-old cronuts. (I would eat a week-old cronut for the record.)

We talked for over three hours so now I have to somehow navigate my way through all of the audio. Maybe Grady will let us turn the *Centennial* into a biography of Lyle Rainbow. (There is no way for me to fact-check any of this stuff by Friday BTW. Whoops! I guess I'll have to believe Lyle that he got the ass whooping of the century outside a Duluth Taco Bell.)

In other news, I texted Alex "Thanx" around 11:30 last night and we got into an hour debate about the importance of upholding grammar in all communication. HOW DID I EVER DATE THAT GUY? And then date him again. And then again. We have a real Ross and Rachel thing going on but we're both Ross. Gross.

Should I try to sleep with Coralee tonight? I think so too. Byeeeee!

G

4:15 PM

Do you have access to a television?

Ha!

No.

But I do have access to all of my exes' Hulu accounts.

One of my jokes is gonna be on the show tonight!

WHAT

HOW

WHAT IS IT

I made a joke about that state senator who used his GoFundMe to buy a nicer house and one of the writers overheard it, pitched it in the room and then GAVE ME CREDIT

So everyone knows it's my joke!

Holy shit. I can't believe a writer gave someone else credit.

I KNOW

I'm freaking out!

Is Ben happy?

Um . . . I think he's happy but a little miffed.

Y? Has he never gotten a joke on-air?

Correct.

Ugh. Men.

It's not a men thing! It's a people thing!

Lacie "bumped" me in the bathroom. I don't think it was an accident.

Weird. I don't think I experience jealousy.

FALSE!

You don't experience ROMANTIC jealousy.

But you do experience PROFESSIONAL jealousy.

How so?

I don't have enough time to tell you.

I'm not a jealous person.

You're certainly a DELUSIONAL person.

And soon to be grandmother of 3 to 5 cats!

We're both growing a lot.

THE FRAGILITY OF THE MALE EGO AND OTHER OCCURRENCES

 Ava Helmer <AVA.HELMER@gmail.com>   10/10/19

to Gen

Pardon my subject line, but I'm a bit riled! Ben and I were supposed to grab dinner tonight, and once I found out about my joke getting on the show, I suggested somewhere "$$" instead of "$" on OpenTable. Ben played dumb to our existing plans and told me he couldn't do dinner because he had a stand-up show. At 9PM. Who eats at 9PM in AMERICA? I'm not a Spanish lover for god's sake.

When I suggested getting a quick dinner before the show, he went off on a tirade about my lack of support for his comedy career. He is trying to MAKE something of himself and he would never have gotten into a relationship if he thought I would hold him back from accomplishing his dreams. Do I want him to resent me? Do I?

WOW! It was sort of thrilling to not be the one overreacting for once. I had a bit of an out-of-body experience while he was yelling at me. In public. Like, whoa, no wonder people think I'm crazy. You can't just shout as an adult and get away with it! That's insane!

After he calmed down, I tried to gently inform him that I am not a wicked witch set out to sabotage his dreams of a half-hour Comedy Central special. I was simply asking him to get dinner before his show, which I would like to attend.

Flash forward to me at home alone right now, because I was banned from attending the show. He appreciated my interest but doesn't want to be distracted by our "bad vibes." It's fine. Dana and I are gonna watch Halona say my words as her own in an hour.

I think Ben might suck . . . Does Ben suck?

A

11:14 PM

HAHAHAHAHAHAHA

THAT'S A GOOD JOKE

Thank you :)!!!

You should write more jokes.

Good idea!

Also, Ben sucks.

When will the clip go up? I want to retweet it every day until I die.

hahahaha tomorrow

Perfect 👍

Ben sucks.

Fri, Oct 11, 10:42 AM

I turned another one!

Is this Tabby?

Or have you converted a girl to the dark side?

Hey! Homosexuality is not the dark side!

And it's also not something you can turn someone onto!

Gotcha at your own game!

Fuck.

So what happened??

Details to come.

I have to go cover some Little League upset.

The Barracuda Blues might win this whole thing!

I can't relate to your life anymore.

Me neither.

GIRLS LIKE BOYS (AND GIRLS)

 Gen Goldman <GEN.GOLDMAN@gmail.com> 10/11/19

to Ava

Ah, where to begin? Let me settle into my futon and wax poetic about my own art of seduction. It's a tale as old as Netflix and Chill. After some flirty banter via SMS (because Coralee has a Samsung), the young lady arrived at my very humble abode bearing gifts (wine coolers) and bare skin (jean shorts cutoffs).

Within minutes, we were making out. (I think she had partaken in one or two coolers before arriving.) When I went to take off my pants she started giggling. This was clearly her first below-the-belt same-sex encounter. I asked if she wanted me to stop and in response she took off her pants.

EVERYONE IS GAY! OKAY! WE'RE ALL GAY!*

After I went down on her (SORRY TO BE SO GRAPHIC), she went to the bathroom to pee. Orgasms always make her pee, I guess. (I gave her an orgasm in case that wasn't extremely clear!) When she came back to bed with her pants BACK ON I knew the fun was over. That's okay. She has the rest of her young life to return the favor. And I also have a very powerful vibrator. (AGAIN, APOLOGIES FOR THE GRAPHIC DETAILS. JUST TRY TO BREATHE.)

I wanted her to spend the night, but she had to work in the morning. What does she do? No clue. Forgot to ask. It didn't really occur to me that she exists outside of our warped time together . . . Thinking about her doing mundane things like going to the bank or grocery shopping doesn't really add up . . .

Yes, she is a manic pixie dream girl. But isn't it time the queers got one of those too???

HOW ARE YOUR PARENTS????

If they are reading this email over your shoulder, please see all my apologies for the graphic but necessary details. It's my job as a journalist to disclose the whole truth and nothing but the truth. So help me, Kesha. (Kesha is God.)

GENEVIEVE GOLDMAN, Love Witch

*I know you're not gay. Exception to the rule proves the rule.

Re: GIRLS LIKE BOYS (AND GIRLS)

 Ava Helmer <AVA.HELMER@gmail.com>   10/12/19
to Gen

Ahhh this is all very exciting except the part where she didn't return the favor! I didn't even know you were allowed to do that! Equal rights are crazy.

Will write back more after this weekend! The parents are all fired up and ready to sightsee. Ben has been with us pretty much the whole time. I think my parents actually like him??? I think he's been on best behavior since the stand-up show "incident." Whatever the reason, I'll take it!

G2G SEE N.Y.C. BRB XOXO

A

7:32 PM

Has your dad told any good jokes?
I love your dad's jokes.
He bought a sound machine.

🤖 ????
🤖 It's a little box with all these sounds and he keeps using it in public.
🤖 What kind of sounds????
🤖 Farts.
🤖 Throw up.
🤖 Bomb explosion.
🤖 hahahahahaha
🤖 Love it.
🤖 The public does not.

Sun, Oct 13, 10:12 AM
🤖 Tabby bit me but I think I deserved it.

1:37 PM
🤖 What are you guys doing?????

6:47 PM
🤖 Cool. Cool.
🤖 Me too.

Mon, Oct 14, 9:12 AM
🤖 AHHH I'm sorry.
🤖 My parents took over my every waking moment!
🤖 They just left for the airport.

GEN!

I'm sorry!!!

OK.

Please don't punish me!

I'm not punishing you. But I did some bad things because you left me to my own devices for an entire weekend.

Oh, no.

How bad?

I booked a plane ticket for D.C.

RUNNING FOR CONGRESS BAD???

Ha! I've missed our banter.

I'm going to visit Alex.

Whyyyyyyy

He makes you sad!

I have to feel something!

It's so hot down here my whole body is numb!

That can't be true!

Please get a physical.

Like I would trust a Florida doctor!

IT HAPPENED ONE WEEKEND

 Ava Helmer <AVA.HELMER@gmail.com>   10/14/19
to Gen

Dearest Genevieve,

Let me take this moment to reiterate my deepest apologies regarding my absence this weekend. As previously texted, my mother and father were QUITE demanding of my time and energy. I don't know if you remember this, but they are a HOOT! My mom has started doing barre classes and insisted on keeping up her stamina despite the trip, ergo, we all had to go to a barre class. That's right! Me, my mom, my dad AND Ben. My dad wore jeans. So just take a moment to think about my dad in a barre class WEARING JEANS. Afterwards he kept bragging about how easy it was, but that's because he couldn't do any of it!

Ben was a real trooper. And not just while sweating next to my inflexible parents. He was with us ALL weekend. He showed us around and we went to one of his shows. He mentioned his GIRLFRIEND in his set. It wasn't an actual story about me (he reused it from an old relationship) but at least he's publicly acknowledging his lack of singleness!

He and my dad got along great because he has a basic knowledge of baseball. My mom was more reserved but I think she's hung up on the whole "he's my boss" thing because she's a 1970's second-wave feminist so she looks down on using your sexuality to get ahead. Very old-school thinking. (Are you proud of my ability to dissect feminism? College was worth it!)

They kept asking about you BTW. My mom loved your Open All Doors piece and she read Lyle's profile before I did! She pointed out a few potential discrepancies in his story. Why she did not become an editor I will never know.

Anyway, I'm the happiest I've ever been! This can't last, right? Something really bad is coming? Do you think it's going to be a natural disaster? I would feel so guilty if I caused a natural disaster!

LOVE AND FAMILIA,

AVA

P.S. Have you talked to your parents at all? My mom asked and I didn't know the answer. . . . EMBARRASSING! Clearly failing on my best-friend inquiries. I vow to do better!

Re: IT HAPPENED ONE WEEKEND

 Gen Goldman <GEN.GOLDMAN@gmail.com> 10/14/19
to Ava

Your dad went to a barre class in jeans??? Ken! What a trendsetter! I'm only wearing jeans to work out now in solidarity (good thing I don't work out). I can't believe you didn't document this with a photo or at least a Boomerang! I love Boomerangs!

Sounds like a pretty PG weekend. You must have been in hog heaven! (I say things like *hog heaven* now because of the South.) I too had a rather PG weekend but not for lack of trying. Alex refuses to sext with me because of the NSA. The NSA doesn't care if we sext!! It is so annoying being in love with an aspiring politician. What's the point of living if you don't get caught in some sort of lurid sex scandal?

Turns out Alex is just as bored and lonely in D.C. as I am in gator town. He didn't admit that, of course, because that would imply self-awareness and emotional intelligence. But it's pretty obvious he hasn't clicked with any of the other assistants. It's probably due to his off-putting personality. Man, do I love a nut that's hard to crack. TBH I've never met a nut I don't love. Take that as you will.

Feeling a bit of scoop withdrawal this morning. I want to expand the Open All Doors investigation, but I don't really know where to go from here. Maybe I'll reach out to some local politicians. Get them to publicly condemn the policy. A girl can dream . . .

I leave for D.C. in T-minus four days. Do you think I will stick out now that I exclusively wear Hawaiian shirts??

GODSPEED,

G

4:27 PM

Excuse me.

Si?

You dodged my P.S. about your parental units.

Gen can't come to the phone right now, she is investigating what a local bear did during the hours of 2 and 5 AM.

What? Why?

Because a campsite got ruined and Gen needs to get to the bottom of it!

Stop referring to yourself in the third person!

I think the bear lost his lover to a bigger bear and was eating his sorrows.

We've all been there.

So you haven't talked to them at all?

The bears? No. Not yet.

You have to talk to your parents, Gen.

Y?

Eh. Good point.

Tell your parents to adopt me and I'll talk to them constantly.

On it!

WARNING: PARANOIA

 Ava Helmer <AVA.HELMER@gmail.com>   10/15/19
to Gen

Hello,

It's me, Ava. I'm standing on the edge of an emotional cliff, asking you to stop me from jumping. What is making me want to jump, you ask? A sneaking suspicion that everything I thought about Ben is not true and he is about to leave me for someone else.

What evidence do I have? None. Except my gut. And we all know how powerful a tool my weak Jewish stomach is.

A BRIEF HISTORY OF AVA'S GUT

1) Fourth grade. Everyone in my class wanted to get into that guy's van. I didn't. Luckily the teachers intervened and that man was arrested.

2) Seventh grade. I didn't go to Katie Lippert's sleepover because I thought something bad would happen. Something bad DID happen. Lucy Forlini went into anaphylactic shock. True, no one else was harmed. But a lot of those girls had minor PTSD from seeing their friend suffocating.

3) All of high school. I knew Principal Weaver was a bad guy. BOOM. Pedophile. Called it. (Not the pedophilia per se but the general creepiness.)

4) Three summers ago. I tried to warn you that that girl was two-timing you. You told me you were also two-timing her so it was fine. But then . . . She had a secret kid! You didn't know about the secret kid, did you?? No. You didn't! BOOM.

5) Kevin Spacey.

Per above, I think we can agree that my suspicions about Ben are most likely true and I should prepare myself for the inevitable mental breakdown. Good thing I have therapy tonight! Maybe I can just check myself into the psych ward now and save us all some time.

OH GOD WHY?

A

3:18 PM

Where are you?

In hell.

Where are you physically?

In the intern cubicle.

You guys have to share a cubicle? Aren't there like ten of you?

Are you trying to make me feel worse????

No! Sorry!

What is going on?

Nothing. I just have a feeling.

He's being cold.

Aren't you at work?

Maybe he just has work to do?

LIKE WHAT??? HOOK UP WITH ANOTHER INTERN???

Ava, nothing has happened.

You forgot to include all the times your gut was WRONG in that email.

Name one time!

Tom Hanks.

It just hasn't come out yet! No one is that nice!

When is therapy?

7.

Promise me you won't do anything rash before then.

Define rash.

An eruption or efflorescence on the skin.

Too late! I have hives all over my neck.

Damn.

Send pic.

I'M CURED!

 Ava Helmer <AVA.HELMER@gmail.com>   10/15/19
to Gen

Just kidding. Mental illness is a lifestyle, baby! You're in it for LYFE! Unless it's postpartum depression. That's pretty time-period specific. Although I'm not sure if the effects ever fully go away. That will be a good thing to look up when I can't sleep later.

Dr. Grimm talked me down from the ledge. We realized that what I'm most scared about isn't losing Ben but losing my balance. I've been doing so well since I've moved to New York and a (large) part of me feels like it's too good to be true. It's almost like I have imposter syndrome for just living a normal life. Like I'm not wired to be happy so something must be terribly wrong? Ben is the most unexpected part of my new life so it makes sense that I don't trust it. She encouraged me to keep my fears and anxieties to myself instead

of trying to solve or catch something. I have to give
him space to be a person and show me who he
really is.

NY therapists are GOOD! Despite NYU's suicide rates
(very high).

Dana and I are off to see a late movie! Look at
me missing my self-imposed curfew like a normal
young adult! I'm a real girl! (I meant that as a reference
to Pinocchio in case it mistakenly reads as
transphobic.)

LOVE YOU TO THE LGBT CENTER AND BACK! (Do
they even have those in Florida?)

A

11:35 PM
Dr. Grimm for the win!
What movie did you see?
Were there any queer characters?
It was a kids' movie . . .
SO!
SO!!
I have to go to sleep.
But I'm bored!
Write a think piece.
About the underrepresentation of queer
characters in children's media?
ON IT!

AND THE PLOT THICKENS

 Gen Goldman <GEN.GOLDMAN@gmail.com> 10/16/19

to Ava

It's finally happened. After only a little over a month at *The Fernandina Beach Centennial* I have made my first enemy! Took longer than normal. Although I suspect I was just slow on the uptake and he has been plotting my demise for weeks!

Who shall try to cross me? None other than the heir to the throne! Beau Adams of House Adams. Editor-in-Chief Grady's pride and joy! I shall defeat you! House Goldman might have tarred its name with scandal upon scandal but we are nothing if not scrappy! A Goldman never pays her debts but she does ruin her enemies with slander!

What has Beau Adams of House Adams done? Why, he's stifled a story! And not just any story about water-balloon fights or egg-slinging bandits, but the greatest story of the last ten years! (Collusion with Russia notwithstanding.) He has put the kibosh on any additional Open All Doors coverage! And to what end? To push his competition for heir out of the way!

But seriously, he totally went behind my back and got in Grady's ear. He convinced him that too many advertisers are congregants of the church and we shouldn't press our luck. So I'm not allowed to ask any congressmen or local officials about it.

What the actual fuck, Beau? You're a goddamn copy editor who can barely spell! Don't come at me with business advice. He's clearly pissed that his father likes me more than him. It's not my fault everyone likes me! I have an air of defiance. People are naturally drawn to that.

LONG PATHETIC STORY SHORT, I am now going to make it my life's mission to get Beau fired from his father's paper. That's right! I'm ripping the American family apart just like they thought the homosexuals would!

My plan of attack: self-destruction. Let him build his own grave. And then I'll give him a friendly push. MAN! I miss having an enemy. Really gets the blood going.

I thought about bringing Cash (unpaid, closeted intern) on board but I don't think I should involve him in office politics. Aren't you proud? I'm being so mature about this whole thing!

Winter Is Coming,

Genevieve of House Goldman

Re: AND THE PLOT THICKENS

 Ava Helmer <AVA.HELMER@gmail.com>   10/16/19
to Gen

Wow. A lot of *Game of Throne* references. I think I understood most of them. (HOW DO YOU TELL ALL THE STARKS APART??? I SURE CAN'T!)

I'm glad your "blood is boiling" again but maybe you should wait a few months before attempting to take down the "heir to the throne." Although it is really annoying that you have to drop the story. My mom will be especially disappointed.

Things are a lot less passive-aggressive and more overtly aggressive over here in the entertainment industry. One of our segment producers just got fired for stealing some kid's format from YouTube. (Dressing kids up as adults to try to buy guns.) *People* magazine happened to be doing a feature on Halona so she made a big speech about plagiarism and not stealing "from the youth." I'm pretty sure that YouTube channel is run by like, middle-aged ex-*SNL* writers, but you know, digital. It's for the kids!

The big takeaway here is that I might appear in the background of a *People* magazine photo spread, cowering in the corner and carrying a tray of muffins. FAME HAS CHANGED ME!

The other takeaway is a segment producer job is up for grabs, which means another, more attainable position might open if they hire from within. Everyone thinks it's gonna go to this junior producer, Shayna. Shayna used to be an intern . . . So you know what that means! Fight to the death! Or they hire someone more experienced from the outside and everything stays the same. TBD.*

*My entire life.

AVA, as seen in the background of *People* magazine

8:45 PM

What is the weather in D.C.?

Low 60s.

Really??

I don't know! I'm not the weather app!

Ughhh. I don't know what to pack.

Perhaps some sort of emotional shield?

Please. This is just one long booty call.

We are NOT getting back together.

I just took a screenshot of this conversation.

To send to you later when you tell me you're back together.

You know how to take screenshots????

FU

Thu, Oct 17, 9:14 AM

You've probably noticed but I haven't talked about Ben in a while. . . .

Define a while? I believe it has been one full day.

That's a long time for an anxious mind!

Did you mean for that to rhyme??

You should patent that!

I don't have time to patent that!

My boyfriend is missing!

Oh no! Maybe he was a ghost the whole time!

What will you do if the security guard tells you there hasn't been a Ben here in forty years . . .

It's New York. Everyone is named Ben.

Touche.

He's not at work and he won't answer my calls or texts.

Ava. Why are those things plural?

When someone is missing you make ONE call and send ONE text.

Otherwise you're immediately a suspect in their disappearance.

Plus you seem really desperate.

He's my BOYFRIEND and he's MISSING!

It's barely even daylight yet.

You're bad in a crisis.

Or am I great?

Bad.

11:52 AM

He's alive.

Damn. I put fifty bucks on ghost.

With who???

Online. You can make all sorts of bets online.

Where was he?

At a doctor's appointment????

Underground???

Oh, cool!!

I'm joking! What doctor doesn't have cell service??

Underground ones! You're coming up with some real clever ideas in distress.

I'm so mad. My face is bright red.

Why are you mad?

Because he ignored me for hours and I thought he was dead!

Right. That's what I thought.

Are you going to confront him?

No. I'm going to handle this with grace.

Shout out to Dr. Grimm.

Shout out to Roxane Gay!

She doesn't get enough shout outs.

I CONFRONTED HIM

 Ava Helmer <AVA.HELMER@gmail.com>   10/17/19

to Gen

And it did not go well. As in, he is no longer my boyfriend and I cried all the way home on the subway. But that has to be some rite of passage, right? Who hasn't cried on the subway! No one even cared! (It might have helped that this guy was taking off his clothes and trying to urinate, but people didn't seem too fazed by that either.)

But let me rewind to a much simpler and less wet (tears! I'm talking about tears!) time.

ROUGHLY TWO HOURS AGO:

OUTSIDE, CITY STREET—EVENING

Pedestrians whizz by on their way to meetings and illicit affairs. A young woman, AVA, rushes out of a high-rise in pursuit of an older man, late 20s, name is not important. (BEN.)

> AVA
> Hey!

The older man turns around, a glimmer of annoyance on his pasty face. He waits.

> AVA
> What happened earlier? Why were you ignoring me?

He lets out a LONG sigh, much longer than natural, definitely forced, very over dramatic.

> OLDER MAN
> I think we want different things.

CUT TO:

Quite a bit of screaming! In public. On the sidewalk. That's two rites of passage in one day! Things are really coming up Ava.

Here are a few highlights from our argument. Please let me know who you think won and who is a pathological liar with a flair for manipulation.

Him: We work together, so this isn't a good idea.
Her: You said it was fine. You convinced me it was fine.

Him: I have to focus on my career.
Her: No one is stopping you from focusing on your career. I come to all your shows.

Him: I just wanted this to be casual. You're moving too fast.
Her: YOU WENT TO A BARRE CLASS WITH MY FAMILY!

Him: Let's just go back to being friends.
Her: WE WERE NEVER FRIENDS!

I await your verdict from inside a pint of ice cream in my bathtub. (Trying to knock out as many rites of passage as possible.)

I KNEW THIS WOULD HAPPEN! ANSWER YOUR PHONE.

A

Re: I CONFRONTED HIM

 Gen Goldman <GEN.GOLDMAN@gmail.com> 10/17/19
to Ava

Ah! I missed your call! And now you're not picking up!
We are star-crossed callers!

Re: Ben!

Are you fucking kidding me??? That bastard! If I had
literally any money I would hop in a 747, fly to New York
and cut one ball off. That's right. Only one. So he
maintains his sex drive but can't have sex until it heals.

Do you remember how you didn't understand what
gaslighting meant? This is gaslighting! He is completely
rewriting your history together and then making you
feel crazy for remembering the truth.

I HATE HIM.

If hell hath no fury like a woman scorned, then double
that for the best friend of that woman. I could rip him
apart with my bare hands. And then smear his insides
on Beau's model train collection.

The only good thing to come out of this is proof of your
psychic abilities. You might be one more notch on his
bedpost but he's another bullet point in A Brief History
of Ava's Gut. If this whole writing thing doesn't work
out, the CIA would be lucky to have you.

Please don't let this bring you (all the way) down! You have so much going for you! You still have an incredible internship and a surprisingly nice roommate. Your parents are rich AND supportive. And I'm your best friend. In the rankings of best life ever it's pretty much Cardi B and then you. Call me back when you can so I can hear your melodious high-pitched voice.

All my love and rage,

G

7:45 PM

Are you still alive?

Yes.

Unfortunately.

Where are you?

My room.

Have you contacted him?

Why?

What did you say?

Stuff.

AVA!

Other people do hard drugs! I send regrettable texts! Leave me alone!

Fair.

But I'm never going to leave you alone.

8:13 PM

How am I supposed to go in to work tomorrow???

I want to die.

He's just a guy!

There will be many more guys!

And, maybe, if you're open, a lady or two.

SAY HELLO TO MY LITTLE FRIEND

 Gen Goldman <GEN.GOLDMAN@gmail.com> 10/18/19

to Ava

I am officially catfishing Beau. That's right. I have created a new identity based on all of Beau's interests: boobs, blondes, fishing and candles. Yep! He loves candles, especially musky ones. They stink up the whole office! This place is going to be so much better once I destroy him.

Her name is Beulah Bottoms and she lists her birthday as 1985 but she doesn't look a day over thirty. I found, courtesy of Google, images for the keywords "tragic accidents." Don't worry. I only used the *before* photos.

I wanted to start small to keep it believable but Beau took the bait so easily, Beulah's been chatting with him all morning on Facebook Messenger! It's like he's never even heard of a bot.

Full confession, I'm not totally sure how Beulah will cause his professional demise but I am desperately in need of something to do (other than my job). I leave for the airport in three hours so Beulah will be offline for the weekend. That will certainly drive him wild!

How are you doing??? Other than alive. I'm choosing to believe you are still alive.

LOVE YOU INSIDE AND OUT AND ALSO INSIDE,

G

4:32 PM

How are you getting to D.C.?

Air Force One.

How are you paying for it?

Alex hooked me up with miles.

It's good to bang people in moderate places.

He might dominate me financially but I wear the strap-on.

You know what I mean????

AVA???????

6:32 PM

On the plane.

Safe flight.

Are you okay?

Yeah.

BIG BOYS STOMPING IN MY AIR FORCE ONES

 Gen Goldman <GEN.GOLDMAN@gmail.com> 10/19/19
to Ava

D.C. is crazy. I thought all of America was crazy, but these crazy people actually influence things, which makes it even scarier. Every single person in the airport was wearing a suit. Except my flight. (Florida! Keeping it casual! Regardless of the circumstances or appropriateness!)

I took a cab to Alex's apartment. He offered to pick me up, but I like to be low-maintenance. Plus it's always fun to maintain an element of surprise. I wanted to barge in naked but he double-locked his door and has a roommate so that plan went out the window. I actually really like his roommate, Simone. She doesn't speak but you can tell she's thinking.

I thought we would spend the night in, because, you know, sex, but Alex wanted to "show me the city," which meant he needed to network at some event. Fine! Whatever! I am great at schmoozing. But apparently I'm NOT great at dressing myself. Alex went through my suitcase and determined NONE of my two outfits were "business casual." WHY WOULD THEY BE??? If I ever do any business I want to be very formal about it.

He ended up asking his roommate to dress me, which led to a very unforgettable nude session where I bared my chest and Simone faced the wall. I ended up in a pencil skirt and blazer. I would send you a photo but I wouldn't let anyone take any.

The "networking" occurred in some fancy hotel lobby and I got "too drunk" so now Alex is ignoring me and I'm eating hash browns from McDonald's. Feels like college!

I think you'd like D.C. It's very clean. Although I'm told there is a "dirty side." Maybe we should both live here and move to the appropriate quarters for our personality/hygiene.

Alex just made eye contact for the first time all morning so I've got to run!

Miss you! Love you! Wouldn't want to be you!*

GEN

*Unless it was only for like a day. That could be dope.

3:25 PM

Look at my Instagram

Why?

Because it's funny.

And I love attention!

5:12 PM

Are we in a fight?

Because I know I can be a bit oblivious but I don't remember a fight.

Except for the five or six ones I've already had with Alex.

He is my favorite person to fight with.

Is this why people get married?

7:37 PM

Let's just talk when you're back. Have a fun weekend.

WOW!!!!

Is this how you treat the guys you date????

It's ruthless!

8:21 PM

What did I do????

You have to tell me so I can prepare my defense!

Stop it. You're with Alex.

No! I'm with his colleagues. Alex is nowhere to be seen.

????

Oh! There he is! He went to the bathroom.

I'm drunk.

I know.

I LOVE YOU
BUT I'M NOT SORRY
You don't even know what you did!
Yeah, but I hate taking responsibility! So
I'm getting out in front of this one.
Tell Alex to get you a water.
You take such good care of me.

HERE'S THE THING

Ava Helmer <AVA.HELMER@gmail.com>   10/20/19

to Gen

I'm pissed. At first I thought maybe I was being too sensitive since I'm going through a breakup. But then I realized I AM GOING THROUGH A BREAKUP and you, my best friend, don't seem to give a shit.

I already know what you're going to say in response to this.

1) People break up all the time. It's not that big of a deal.

MY RESPONSE: Sure. But not everyone is me, a mentally unstable headcase who puts far too much importance on romantic relationships. Do I want to be this way? Absolutely not. Do I know how to stop being this way? Absolutely not. So even if YOU don't think it's a big deal, it is a big deal to ME.

2) Ben sucks. This is a good thing.

MY RESPONSE: You have never met him. You don't actually know him. Us staying together and being HAPPY would have been the good thing.

3) Don't want to dwell on the bad. Better to move on as quickly as possible.

MY RESPONSE: I need time to process and grieve. Also it's been less than a WEEK.

I'm sorry if this is aggressive but you asked me so I figured I'd tell you the truth. We obviously don't need to get into it all right now. Tell Alex I say hi.

A

10:07 PM
- You get back okay?
- Yep.
- Did you see my email?
- Yep.
- Cool. So glad I took the time to write it.

Re: HERE'S THE THING

 Gen Goldman <GEN.GOLDMAN@gmail.com> 10/22/19

to Ava

Hey, sorry I didn't get back to you sooner. Things ended badly with Alex so I sort of took the day off from people yesterday. (If by some chance Grady calls you, the official story is food poisoning from those shady politicians. The true story is I spent the entire day watching *Madam Secretary* because there are two bi characters in season three and I had to start from the beginning for context.)

While I appreciate you taking the time to answer for me, I would prefer to speak for myself from now on.

I'm sorry you're hurting. But I can't just drop everything in my life whenever you go through a breakup. I'm not saying the breakups are always your fault but it's hard for me to see you date the same kind of guy over and over again. You are a catch, Ava! But not everyone is smart enough to see that.

Also, I'm just getting a bit tired with the whole "I need a guy to be happy" thing. I get why you want it but you don't NEED it. You have a kickass job, you're living in N.Y.C. and you don't even enjoy sex that much. Why not focus on the good stuff and not some shitty stand-up comedian twice your age? (That was an exaggeration obviously but come on, we are nowhere near thirty. It's like another galaxy.)

Sorry if this is aggressive but I also wanted to be honest.

G

9:32 PM

What happened with Alex?

Is this your version of an olive branch?

No.

I'm still mad.

But I'm also nosy and curious.

Ah! A juicy story!

Or as I call them, "Ava's kryptonite!"

If I had to pick ONE thIng that went wrong I guess I would have to say his personality.

He has a bad one.

hahaha

Has D.C. changed him?

No. He is the same.

HA!

I guess we both keep making the same mistake, huh?

Yeah, but mistakes are my brand. You're supposed to be the smart one.

You did better on the SATs . . .

WHEN ARE YOU GOING TO LET THAT GO! I GUESSED HALF THE ANSWERS!

THAT MAKES IT WORSE!

ur unbearable

I'm so glad we're friends again.

THE PROBLEM WITH PEOPLE

 Gen Goldman <GEN.GOLDMAN@gmail.com> 10/22/19

to Ava

And by people, I mean Alex. What is with that guy??? Has he always been an unbearable mix of arrogance and cluelessness? Don't answer that.

I honestly thought it would be a fun, carefree weekend. You know, because we are twenty-two and the world is burning, so why not enjoy ourselves? Apparently, there is no "fun" in Washington, D.C., and to assume so only shows my "ignorance." Which is surprising because I "claim to be an active citizen of the world."

BLAH BLAH BLAH BLAH BLAH

I finally figured out where he actually works, by the way. It's called ACORE and it's a lobby that promotes green energy. Apparently the clean energy racket is a real toxic environment. Go figure! (Wow. I love puns.) It's very cutthroat and his boss is a real nasty SOB despite living a completely sustainable lifestyle. I asked if he would ever switch causes, maybe work for the National Center for Trans Equality, where the people might be nicer and he SNAPPED. How could I not realize by now that being trans isn't his entire identity? Do I not listen to him AT ALL?

In my defense, everyone knows I'm a bad listener.

I'm also pretty sure he's never mentioned a passion for clean energy before . . . I think it just looks good on his resume. But what do I know? I'm just a political wife.

We also argued over my meat intake. Actual meat. He's vegan now. If that wasn't completely obvious from everything I said above. Something about eating a lot of beans brings out the worst in people.

It was such a relief to come home to my pregnant cat. Lyle Rainbow watched her while I was gone since I needed a cat sitter and he needed a home. I think that lady is going to pop any day now but I also have no idea how cat pregnancy works . . .

Long story short, I am in love with Alex and will not stop until he is mine again.

Planes, Trains and Super Shuttles,

Ms. Genevieve Goldman

Re: THE PROBLEM WITH PEOPLE

 Ava Helmer <AVA.HELMER@gmail.com>   10/23/19
to Gen

Can I start out by saying: you are insane. And that is coming from someone who publicly identifies as crazy.

YOU ARE NOT IN LOVE WITH ALEX.

You are in love with a challenge. Because you come from a broken home and your father never gave you love unless you begged for it. (Pretty good analysis, right?)

I understand that Alex *appears* to be a catch. He is handsome, driven and incredibly smart. He also SUCKS to be around. Remember when I came to visit you senior year and he wouldn't let us talk over *Vanderpump Rules* because "talking ruins the viewing experience?" It was freaking *VANDERPUMP RULES*! Talking over it *is* the viewing experience!

He is also pretty mean to you and I think sometimes you think it's his way of flirting but he's just being mean . . .

You told me to stop making the same mistakes. I think you need to listen to your own advice for once. (About this situation specifically. Do NOT listen to any of your other advice. Next thing I know all your money will be tied up in Bitcoin. Sometimes I'm glad you don't have any money to lose . . .)

I would keep yelling but I have to get back to work. Now that Ben is no longer interested in giving me a "leg up," I have to actually get to know everyone else in the office or else I have no shot at the junior producer position. I keep kicking myself for not turning my bizarre lunch with Halona into more of a career opportunity.

But as that old saying goes: you live, you learn, you die.

Ava

Guess what!

Chicken butt!

I want a divorce.

Fine. But I get the house AND the kids.

I should never have agreed to the prenup!

What happened??

Beau wants to meet Beulah IRL!

What? Who is Beulah!???

The perfect woman!

Beulah Bottoms!

Ohhhh the catfish!

Beau has been sending her love messages all weekend!

What are love messages???

They're not quite sexts but they're not platonic either!

This is so sad!

What are you going to do now??

Unclear but it's gonna be huge.

OY.

HOW TO GET BOTTOMS INTO BEAU'S ASS

Gen Goldman <GEN.GOLDMAN@gmail.com> 10/23/19

to Ava

Sorry. I couldn't resist.

I honestly completely forgot about Beulah Bottoms while I was in D.C. but I had given Lyle the login info so Beau's future lover wouldn't totally disappear for days. I thought he would maybe check in once or twice but this guy went full-blown John Adams. (Adams was known for sending tender and lengthy correspondences to his wife, Abigail. Wanted to save you the google. Unless you want to actually read those letters. Which I can't recommend enough.)

Lyle and Beau have been sending paragraphs upon paragraphs to each other. I had no idea Beau was such a fan of war novels. He has read every one. About every war. This seems like a pretty big red flag to me but Lyle (pretending to be Beulah) loved it? Why do boys love war so much? I guess we will never know. But it's one more argument for the matriarchy.

I haven't been this excited since Tegan and Sara performed at Emerson and Tegan winked at me. WHAT IF BEAU AND LYLE FALL IN LOVE??? WHAT IF THIS WAS MY PURPOSE ON THIS EARTH??? Fuck journalism, I am going to create some sort of catfish/matchmaking service. I have to see if fishmatch.com is already taken!

Beau is getting real eager to plant a wet one on Beulah
Bottoms's bottom so we need to come up with an
excuse. Here are our options thus far:

1) Botox gone wrong. Needs time for skin to heal.

2) Caring for an ailing parent who can't be left alone in
case they need to defecate.

3) Agoraphobia.

4) Currently traveling for international work that may or
may not involve illegal espionage.

5) Bad belly.

I eagerly await your thoughts. I am leaning towards 2.
Lyle votes 4.

G

7:52 PM
Botox gone wrong.
But that's so boringgggg.
Which makes it believable!
What did you mean by "bad belly"?
General badness that causes inability to
leave the home.
Sticking with Botox.
FINE.

8:11 PM

I haven't brought up Ben in days BTW.

I know!

I haven't brought him up either!

FALLING OFF THE OL' WAGON

Ava Helmer <AVA.HELMER@gmail.com>   10/24/19

to Gen

Okay, so I know I literally JUST bragged about not talking about Ben, but I have to bring him up because I HATE him. Guess who went to lunch with Halona today? Lacie. Guess why? Because Ben set it up. Is he already fucking Lacie? Unclear. Is he the biggest dick I have ever met? Absolutely. And I do NOT mean that in the physical way. He was average at best. And I am never having sex again because it only leads to bad things. And minor stinging if I don't use enough lube.

This whole thing is ridiculous because Lacie doesn't even LIKE Ben. And she was pissed at me for getting special treatment. (Hypocrite, much?) I think the worst part of all this is how DUMB I feel. I've always been bad at boys but I've never been bad at work. The only thing that kept me going was knowing I would have my success to keep me warm when I went to bed alone at night. Now I have nothing! And our radiator is barely working so it is very cold! My pinky toe feels like it's going to fall off! If that happens I'll be alone, unsuccessful and lopsided. The pinky toe does a lot more than you think!

The only sliver of good that has come out of this is my repaired relationship with Dana. He took really good care of me post-breakup. He didn't make me talk about it when I was scream-crying in my room but he keeps bringing me snacks and inviting me places. Plus, he's totally giving Lacie the cold shoulder now, which feels way better than it should.

Question: if you are mature, do you just not have feelings? Or do you only feel happy things? Like joy? What does joy feel like?

I hate Ben. Ben all men. Do you get it? Ben instead of ban. (That will be my sign for Women's March 2019.)

A

2:32 PM

Oh my god.

I know, right??

How do you know?

Did you read my email?

Not yet!

Oh . . .

What are you "oh my god"ing?

Beau is looking up summaries of war novels on his computer!

I don't think he actually reads them!

Lyle is going to be heartbroken.

Lyle knows this isn't a real relationship, right?

I think so.

I'll ask him when I get home.

HE STILL LIVES WITH YOU????

What am I going to do? Throw him out?

He's Tabby's father!

I guess it's important for a cat to have two parents.

EXACTLY!

3:10 PM

WOW!

BEN IS AN ASSHOLE

Thank you for reading.

8:12 PM

Should Dana and I start a YouTube channel together?

What kind of channel?

I'll probably say yes regardless.

Something comedic.

Maybe like our own version of Weekend Update? But we are playing characters? Who don't understand the news?

So regular news anchors?

JK

I love it!

Really??

For sure. You need a project.

 Other than me.

 Awww, you'll always be my favorite project.

 I reject your need to fix me!

 But I also love the attention.

BREAKING NEWS

Gen Goldman <GEN.GOLDMAN@gmail.com> 10/25/19

to Ava

Isn't it ironic that I'm actually supposed to be covering breaking news and instead I'm sending emails to you during work hours?! Jobs are crazy!

I have two very important items to report.

1) Coralee is officially "in a relationship" on Facebook with someone named Deacon Mason who looks like he can bench 250 and also forgot to vote but if he did it would have been for Gary Johnson. He seems to love rifles and his mom. (Basing this off of a massive back tattoo that involves both a rifle and the word "Mom." I have no idea how she met this guy or how long they have been "unofficial" before now. If I had to "check in" with my feelings about the situation per your endless meddling I would say I feel "highly amused." The guy's name is Deacon Mason! Coralee wouldn't go that hard at being straight if she wasn't at least a little bit queer.

She will be crawling back to me in no time! (I realize bisexuality exists, as I am a notable and long-standing member of the community, but give me this.)

2) Beau is a changed man. He smiles at me at least half the time we make eye contact and he seems to be showering more. I think he's actually been whistling while going to the bathroom. (It's a painfully cramped office. I'm a bit worried about Phyllis's bowels if we're being honest.) I think now is the perfect time to cuddle up to him metaphorically and make him change his mind about cutting off my Open All Doors exposé. I need to do it quickly before the entire catfish plot blows up in my face. Because I really don't see a way out of this one . . . Unless Beulah Bottoms gets killed off . . . That always seems to solve plot problems on TV shows. Also great if the actor gets pregnant or needs to go to rehab. REHAB! Maybe Beulah goes to rehab! Wow! Sometimes you just need to talk/write things out.

Those are my updates! Also, Alex texted me but I'm trying not to care enough to make it an official update. Especially since it was just a link to an article about the health hazards of too much sugar. We haven't talked in a week and he sends me an article about the health hazards of sugar! That man is a maniac! I love him.

More news at 10.

JK

I am very bored!

G

Re: BREAKING NEWS

 Ava Helmer <AVA.HELMER@gmail.com>   10/25/19
to Gen

I no longer believe these are people's actual names.
Deacon Mason??? Come on! I'm on to you and your
elaborate exaggerations. I bet his name is Dan Mason
or something . . . Maybe there isn't even a new BF
after all . . . Maybe Coralee is a figment of your twisted
imagination! Maybe you aren't even in Florida!

If you didn't look so tan in your IG pics, I would fly
down there and try to expose you!

Assuming the rest of your news update was real, I have
to say you are really taking everything in stride.
Although I wouldn't assume Coralee will come crawling
back. Maybe you should get back on the apps? And
meet someone new? (I'm purposely not engaging
about the Alex "update" if you can even call it that.
DOES HE HAVE FEELINGS? HOW CAN WE
SURVIVE WITHOUT SUGAR?)

Re: Beau. I think Botox followed by rehab makes sense
for character development. She clearly has no problem
injecting things into her body! Ba dam tss! I
recommend getting out of this con as quickly as
possible. I don't think I need to explain why.

Things are really heating up over here between Ben
and Lacie. I caught them chatting at the water cooler
because my life is a parody of cliché heartbreak. They

both looked at me with so much pity, which FOR ONCE I don't think I earned.

Never let me shit where I eat again, okay?

I'm gonna bathe my wounds in frozen hot chocolate later with Dana and some of his UCB friends. I dropped the ball on signing up for the class because of a boy (and my crippling fear of performing in public). I might do a boot camp for the first level so I can catch up with Dana.

How is your pregnant cat? Are you giving her multivitamins?

AVA HELMER, a reformed idiot

8:13 PM

Guess who texted me.

Weed.

hahaha

You think marijuana, the plant, texted me?

I am on marijuana

I can tell!

Obama

Ha! I wish!

What do you think Obama texts about?

Dogs.

I would KILL to text Obama about dogs.

Woof!!

Is someone there to take care of you bb?

Woof!!

That's dog for yes!

Who texted??

Coralee!

Shut the fuck up!

Already???

MY LOVE IS HER DRUG

I can't stop eating.

Woof!

THE CURIOUS CASE OF CORALEE

 Gen Goldman <GEN.GOLDMAN@gmail.com> 10/26/19

to Ava

How ya doing weed head? I'm assuming you got home safe and sound and then ate yourself into oblivion? If so: proud of you.

I thought I'd take another stab at filling you in since you kept barking at me last night. (Which I loved. Obviously.)

Coralee reached out around 8 last night with a simple, "Hey, what you up to?" Interesting move since she recently went public with the boy she never mentioned before. In an effort to be the more honest and forthcoming one, I replied, "Clipping my toenails and watching *Queer Eye* with Lyle." No response. I caved and followed up with "What u doing?" She replied, "Bored. Watching the BF play video games."

I WALKED RIGHT INTO HER TRAP!

She got to casually mention her BF like it was no big deal. There is no way she would have gotten away with that shit if I was a guy she was hooking up with. Sure, us queer ladies can get married and walk around holding hands (in most parts of the country) but there is still a HUGE double standard when hooking up with "straight girls." She's lucky I'm not a psycho. Or at least, not a psycho about this stuff. Don't try to come at me about politics.

Instead of confronting the elephant in the room named Deacon Mason (hahahahahah), I simply asked, "What game?" Because I am the MASTER.

Within half an hour we were sexting while Deacon progressed to level 5 of BioShock 2. I'd feel bad for the guy if I hadn't seen his back tattoo.

How was your night, you stoner????

G, Master of Ceremonies and Mind Games

Re: THE CURIOUS CASE OF CORALEE

 Ava Helmer <AVA.HELMER@gmail.com>   10/26/19

to Gen

I love weed! It doesn't taste bad and I feel great! Well, not great, but not any worse than usual!

Dana's friends are so great. Except for this one guy, Mickie, who would not stop doing Bill Gates impressions. I think it's the only impression he can do because there is no topical reason to do Bill Gates . . . I guess it is the price I have to pay for hanging out with improvisors.

For at least an hour, I completely forgot about Ben and his bad stand-up. I never told you this but it was BAD. Like cringe-worthy. I think I convinced myself it was funny in an "alt" way but it was just dumb and casually racist? Not full-blown or anything, but his sets would have done better in the nineties, before the masses had taste.

I think I'm gonna go sign up for a gym. My therapist recommended it and there is one right around the corner. I don't know what I will do in a gym but it's always good to push yourself? Plus I plan on being high for the majority of my life now and the munchies are going to catch up to me at some point. What if I fall in love at the gym??? (Sorry. I know I shouldn't be doing things based on dumb things like "love" but I can't help it. I'm a romantic! And I need something to motivate me other than exercise.)

What are you going to do today? Please don't say "flirt with Coralee." You're better than being the other woman to some guy. I think you would be good at being the other woman to a really powerful woman, but that's different. I'm not sure why but it seems more interesting and less degrading!

Is there anyone new to focus on? Maybe you should come visit me? We need someone to shut Mickie up!

Toke Up

Ava

5:21 PM

IT'S HAPPENING!

OH MY GOD!

What are you talking about?

BIRTH!

LIFE!

KITTENS!

AHHHHH!!

How many are there??

It hasn't happened yet, but it's coming!

Did her water break?

Do cats have water to break?

I don't think so.

But she keeps licking her genitalia and that's one of the main signs!

Wow. She really is your cat.

8:23 PM

My pussy has stopped licking her pussy.

I think it might have been a false alarm.

Damn!

What am I supposed to do now?

I canceled all my plans for the week!

That can't be true. You don't make plans.

LIFE'S WHAT HAPPENS WHEN YOU'RE BUSY MAKING PLANS BABY

I feel bad for Tabby. You seem like a lot as a roommate.

FALSE ALARM????????

 Ava Helmer <AVA.HELMER@gmail.com>   10/27/19
to Gen

Hello,

How are you? I am not good. I have found what I can only assume is an infected STD on my vulva. I was originally going to write vagina but then I vaguely remembered the vagina is a different part so I googled the female body since sex education in this country is SEVERELY lacking. FOR EXAMPLE, I have never had unprotected sex and yet somehow I have contracted a life-threatening STD!

I know what you're thinking. "Ava, calm down. It's probably an ingrown hair." Believe me, I want nothing more than the culprit to be an ingrown hair. I won't even pull it out. I'll let it grow and grow. I respect hair! I love hair! I think I have AIDS.

Is it possible I'm overreacting due to the recent stress in my (love) life? Sure. Of course! This is classic catastrophizing. BUT I can't help but feel I'm not overreacting. I know I have never been super "in touch" with my body. It took me wayyyy too long to realize I have chronic dry eye. Or realize my daily headaches were *not* normal. I've also misdiagnosed myself with appendicitis more often than I would like to admit. THAT SAID, I am like 99.9 percent sure this is an STD.

If/when I die, please donate my body to science. I want to make at least one important contribution to this world.

All the best,

Ava Helmer, S.T.D.

12:13 PM

It's definitely an ingrown hair.

HOW DO YOU KNOW

Statistics

Do you know how many people have STDS???

A LOT

Send me a photo

Yeah, right.

This is not going into the Cloud.

Have you looked at it using your phone's camera?

Yeah. . . .

Then it's already up there!

How????? I didn't take a photo!

Doesn't matter. They know everything.

I'm not engaging in this. I have to make a doctor's appointment.

For what?

JUST KIDDING YOU DANGEROUS MANIAC

MY LAST WILL AND TESTAMENT

 Ava Helmer <AVA.HELMER@gmail.com> 10/27/19
to Gen

I've had nothing to do all day other than think about my inevitable death so in an effort to think positively, here is what I vow to change if I survive. (It's becoming more and more unlikely so I really aimed high here.)

1) Not feel physically terrible all the time. Why am I tired? No idea but worth figuring out.

    a. Actually eat vegetables. Other than fancy grilled artichokes.

    b. Go to the gym I am now a proud member of.

2) Stop being so negative! I have escaped an untimely death! The least I can do is *try* to enjoy life! For example: if I ever have to wait in a long line, I can use that as a nice time to listen to music or a podcast instead of plotting the murders of everyone in front of me.

3) Get a pet. Most likely one of Tabby's kittens. I am TERRIFIED of fur and shedding. But maybe once I have looked death in the face, a little hair won't seem so bad. Except I wear A LOT of black . . . What are the chances Tabby will have an all-black cat that gravitates toward anxious energy?

4) Be nicer. You get back what you put out, according to this fancy pillow I saw at an overpriced boutique. I don't think I would care about dying as much if I felt I had made more of a positive impact on the people around me.

5) Wear shorts. So what if my legs are pale?! I need to regulate my temperature better in the summer!

6) Bare my truth. Not just in my work but in my relationships. I'm here, I'm crazy, get used to it.

7) TRY an oyster. I don't have to like it, but I can at least try it.

Wow. My list is so boring. Maybe I deserve to die.

A

Re: MY LAST WILL AND TESTAMENT

 Gen Goldman <GEN.GOLDMAN@gmail.com> 10/27/19
to Ava

SYSTEM ERROR YOUR MESSAGE WAS UNABLE
TO BE DELIVERED DUE TO THE LUDICROUSNESS
OF THE CONTENT. PLEASE REWRITE MESSAGE
IN ITS ENTIRETY BEFORE RESENDING.

9:12 PM
That wasn't funny.
Yes it was.

IT'S ALL COMING TOGETHER PERFECTLY

 Gen Goldman <GEN.GOLDMAN@gmail.com> 10/28/19
to Ava

Operation manipulate and destroy Beau is in full
effect. I just cornered him in the kitchen (mini fridge
in a corner) and asked him about his weekend.
He BLUSHED and said he mostly stayed in. (As did
Lyle, aka Beulah Bottoms.) I, not so subtly, brought
up how nice it is to have a home, which segued
nicely into my failed Open All Doors series. A much
more receptive Beau actually listened as I explained the
importance of igniting local change through journalism.

This possibility had clearly never occurred to him before, despite being the son of a newspaper editor . . .

By the end of his cup of coffee, he agreed to talk to Grady about reopening my assignment. Men in love are so malleable! Imagine what I could get him to do if Beulah was real and he was actually getting laid! I could start my own *Spotlight* team!

How is your mental health and ingrown hair?

Gen, International Mastermind

Re: IT'S ALL COMING TOGETHER PERFECTLY

Ava Helmer <AVA.HELMER@gmail.com>   10/28/19

to Gen

My doctor's appointment is in an hour. I asked for a female gyno but I think they're making me see a man. I wish you could come with me. I thought about asking Dana but even I know that's crossing a line. (Thank you social skills class!) I tried to dress extremely conservative to minimize judgement. I want to make it seem like I tripped and fell into an STD. Like, whoops! However did I get here, good sir!

I think I smell. I always smell when I'm nervous. Good thing I don't have an office boyfriend anymore to notice! He hasn't looked at me in days!

I'm glad you're back on the beat but part of me is worried this Beau guy might shoot you and Lyle when he finds out the truth. And knowing Florida, he'll probably not only get away with it, but maybe get some kind of award? Like a key to the city? Or a golden crocodile?

Please be careful. I won't be able to protect you from the grave.

Ava

3:43 PM

I can't believe your ignorance.

Oh no . . . What'd I do now?

Florida awards golden ALLIGATORS, not CROCODILES

Oh shit! Please forgive me. I am but a northern elite (as of two months ago)

Do they really give out golden alligators????

Probably!

Text me after the doctor!

I'll be sending gnarled hair thoughts your way!

5:14 PM

Fuck. Fuck. Fuck. Fuck.

????

5:32 PM

What happened???

6:17 PM

Ava???

What happened?!

What do you think happened??

Alien abduction?

6:20 PM

That was a joke!

POSITIVELY AWFUL

 Ava Helmer <AVA.HELMER@gmail.com>   10/28/19

to Gen

I don't know why I'm even bothering to write this
because my life is so clearly over. I left work early to go
to this gyno that Dana's aunt recommended. Yep! Had
to ask my male roommate to contact his extended family
on behalf of my vagina. I thought it would be some
upscale, Park Avenue spot but the place clearly hadn't
been renovated since we were born. The chairs were
worn and there was coffee on the floor. I tried to tell the
receptionist there was coffee ON THE FLOOR but when
I mentioned it she just rolled her eyes and said, "I know."

WHAT?! Why isn't she cleaning it up? Is it magical coffee that reappears as soon as you clean it up? Have I entered the fourth level of hell? (What are the different hell levels? I'm definitely in one of the worst ones.)

They kept me waiting a good thirty minutes, which was just enough time to convince myself I was definitely dying. I thought about slipping on the spilled coffee on purpose to avoid my appointment completely. But then I realized these freaks wouldn't care if I was covered in coffee. They seem completely unfazed by uncontained coffee.

I'm pretty sure I was visibly shaking by the time an angry nurse called out, "Helmer! A. Helmer!" How hard is it to add "Ava" and make a girl feel welcome??? The nurse had to be sixty-five, which always makes me feel sad. Haven't they worked enough? Will they ever be able to save enough for retirement? Why isn't this doctor paying his staff more?

She introduced herself as "Dr. Klondike's nurse." They are obviously not big on first names at this practice. She asked me if I wanted my mom to come in with me. This was confusing because:

1) My mom is in Los Angeles.

2) I did not come into the office with anyone who could be mistaken for my mother. Mainly because I came in ALONE.

Instead of replying with any of those explanations, I simply said, "I'm okay." Did I mention Dr. Klondike's nurse was TERRIFYING? She started off by asking if I was sexually active. I said, "Not currently but very recently." She rolled her eyes. ARE MOST OF HER PATIENTS NOT SEXUALLY ACTIVE? What strange portal have I entered?

She then asked a series of questions in a monotone that rivaled Ben Stein. (That old guy from the eyedrops commercials.) She finished by inquiring about the purpose for my visit and I whispered, "General checkup and possible infection." She didn't hear me at first because I WHISPERED it so I had to repeat myself in a *slightly* louder voice.

Dr. Klondike's nurse left. Without warning. I was left to put my gown on without any clue if it should open in the front or the back. I decided after much deliberation to have it open in the back. Guess what! That was the wrong decision!

I sat on the exam table freezing my exposed butt off, making a deal with God to never have premarital sex again in exchange for my health. Not even my health exactly. But the absence of any disease that could possibly be my own fault. Cancer? Fine! I'll take it! No one blames your poor decision-making for cancer! (Excluding lung and skin. Oy. Maybe it's better to go with something autoimmune.)

Just when I was bartering my future fertility for the sake of my good name, Dr. Klondike shouted, "Knock knock!" without actually knocking. He took one look at me, laughed, and announced: "How am I going to give you a breast exam with your chest covered and your butt out?!" He then made it worse by informing me I was blushing and then turning to face the corner while I swapped the gown around to open in the front. What is the point of a gown that opens in the front?!

After I changed, like a fool, Dr. Klondike Bar washed his hands, while bragging about having "hot hands." A lot of doctors have "cold hands" but ol' Dr. K has always run warm. So I'm pretty lucky to have him as my doctor. Have I mentioned this man is AT LEAST one thousand years old? Clearly this is a practice where old people go to die while they work!

After swinging my legs up onto the stirrups and scooting down three different times, the following conversation took place:

OLD WARM-HANDED DOCTOR: "Let's just take a looksie . . . Oh."
STUPID AVA MORON: "Oh, what?"
OLD WARM-HANDED DOCTOR: "How old are you?"
STUPID AVA MORON: "Twenty-two. Why? Is every-thing okay?"

STUPID AVA MORON worries that her vagina looks unusually old, which is, coincidentally, a deep-seated fear.

OLD WARM-HANDED DOCTOR: "How long have you had this?"

STUPID AVA MORON can't see what he is referring to because her legs are in stirrups and her eyes are pointed at the ceiling, but her magna cum laude intelligence allows her to infer he is pointing at THE THING.

STUPID AVA MORON: "A couple of days . . . That's actually why I came in . . ."
OLD WARM-HANDED DOCTOR: "So this is your first outbreak?"
STUPID AVA MORON: "OUTBREAK?! So it's . . ."
OLD WARM-HANDED DOCTOR: "I'll have to get a blood test and a fluid sample. But I think we both know what this is."
STUPID AVA MORON: "I don't! I'm not a doctor!"

guttural male laugh that mocks STUPID AVA MORON's very essence

OLD WARM-HANDED DOCTOR: "Let's just get the test results back, sweetheart."

under his breath

OLD WARM-HANDED DOCTOR: "Although this is definitely genital herpes."

The rest of the conversation is a bit of a blur, mainly because I was too busy planning my own demise to listen to him. I know he mentioned something about past sexual partners, and the possibility the virus has laid dormant in my body for years, so I really need to talk to everyone I've EVER been with. He paused here, obviously hoping for me to interject with some sort of defense like, "But I'm a virgin!" or "It has to be this one guy because I've only ever had sex once and it was right before my beloved was shipped off to Iraq." Unfortunately for Warm Hands, I said nothing. Instead, I cried. Loudly. With no care for my reputation because it's already been ruined.

THAT'S MY STORY! You can sell it to the tabloids when I go into hiding.

Ava Herpes, Formerly Helmer

Tue, Oct 29, 8:11 AM

Oh my god

AVA

I just saw your email.

Are you okay??

If you don't respond in the next five minutes I'm calling your mom.

What do you want me to say?

I'll never be okay again.

I'll have to die alone. Probably way too old and alone.

That's better than way too young!

What are you doing right now?

Getting ready for work.

Really?? You don't want to take a sick day?

I will now be sick for the rest of my days.

There is that gallows humor we all know and love!

It's just herpes! Everyone has it!

- Name one person you know who has it.
- Other than you?
- JK JK I am very nervous right now because I know you're upset.
- Oh! My dad's friend from AA. Uncle James. He has it!
- Read what you just wrote! That doesn't make it better!
- I'm sure tons of people we know have it. They just don't say anything.
- Like, I'm sure whoever gave it to you knew they had it but didn't say anything . . .
- According to SVU, that's a punishable crime!
- You're a victim!
- Really?
- Hell, yeah!
- Play that victim card!
- I wish. I have no one to blame but myself.
- Pssh! I never blame myself! And neither should you.
- I have to go to work.
- Are you gonna talk to Ben about it?

JUST A FEW REMINDERS . . .

 Gen Goldman <GEN.GOLDMAN@gmail.com> 10/29/19
to Ava

1) I love you and will always love you. I might not have loved you as quickly as you loved me but I was only like three weeks behind. And if you die first I will love you till I die. That's all I can promise because the afterlife has yet to be proved.

2) This seems like a HUGE deal right now but:

a) Herpes is not life threatening.

b) There are multiple medications to prevent outbreaks.

c) You are not your disease!

d) At least it's not *Epidermodysplasia verruciformis*? Where you turn into a tree! (Look it up.)

3) STD stigma is just that: stigma! There is no reason to attach embarrassment and shame to something as natural as a virus. People get sick all of the time. Why should it matter how or where that disease presents itself?

4) You are still you. Nothing important about your character, your personality or even your body has changed. You'll take whatever medication works best and continue to kick ass!

5) On average, sharks kill ten humans every year. BUT: approximately a hundred people die each year when they are stepped on by cows. That's mostly just a super-fun animal fact but it also serves to remind us just how often our perceptions are not reality.

6) Anyone worth loving won't care about this. And it's not like you enjoy casual sex anyway! Now you'll know someone is truly invested in you before you sleep with them! What a great way to weed out the assholes. More people should get herpes!

7) Fuck the police! Unless they're an elite squad known as the Special Victims Unit. (That's just an evergreen reminder.)

You will get through this. And that's an order!

G

Re: JUST A FEW REMINDERS . . .

 Ava Helmer <AVA.HELMER@gmail.com>   10/29/19
to Gen

Thanks. Now I'm afraid of cows.

3:45 PM

I got sent home.

For having herpes?

They can't do that! Sue the shit out of them!

No one here knows about that.

I got sent home for crying too loudly at my cubicle.

Hold on.

Did you get sent home for crying or crying TOO LOUDLY?

Too loudly.

Someone cries here every day.

Did they ask you what was wrong?

I said someone was sick. And then I blew my nose so much that no one asked any further questions.

What are you going to do with your free day?!

Tell my parents I have brought great shame to their household.

I wouldn't open with that.

Tell me how it goes.

I can already tell you it's not going to go well.

That's the spirit!

YOU'RE AN AUNT!

 Gen Goldman <GEN.GOLDMAN@gmail.com> 10/29/19
to Ava

When one door shuts (not having STDs) another door opens (my cat having kittens)! I came home to find Tabby missing. This is not unusual since she is a free spirit who often hides from me as a form of rebellion. I didn't even bother to look for her at first because Lyle told me that Beau had just requested a nude photo from Beulah and I needed to strategize our next move. But then I heard the tiniest of "meows" and my heart flipped. My babies had arrived. I finally found Tabby and Co. on a pile of clothes in my bedroom closet. She gave birth to three beautiful angels! I have already assigned them names and personalities.

1) **Paul Newman:** calm, cool and collected just like his namesake. Clearly an understated alpha. Has a sensitive side. Will love fish.

2) **James Dean:** the troublemaker of the group. Loves attention. Won't stop until he gets what he wants. Not allowed in a car. Will have to be walked to the vet.

3) **Eartha Kitt:** maternal, loving, sexy as hell. This is the type of feline people write songs about. People will gravitate toward her like they gravitate toward her maternal grandma (me).

Yes, I named my kittens after the most famous

Hollywood threesome of all time. Would you really expect any less?

Cat birth is gross!! A lot of mucus. I think I might just throw out my clothes instead of attempting to wash them. Maybe this is a sign to reinvent my style. What do you think about Bohemian Rocker? I just invented it. I think it might be the new health goth. (Black athleisure wear.)

How are you doing? Do you want me to bike up the coast with my new brood so you can pick a kitty? I think Paul Newman could really bring a calming presence to your life . . .

I BOUGHT A ZOO!

Dr. Genlittle

7:42 PM

⊙ Kittens!!

⊙ When one life ends, three others begin!

⊙ Staaaahp!

⊙ Do you need to take them to the vet?

⊙ ☺

⊙ They seem fine!

⊙ Cats have been having cats for millennia!

⊙ Right? When did mammals start?

⊙ I don't know.

⊙ I went to film school.

⊙ Did you talk to your parents yet?

⊙ I left a message.

What the hell are they doing??

Obviously not sitting around waiting for your phone call!

Rude.

How long ago did you call? They might be pooping.

BOTH OF THEM??

I think if you live together long enough you sync up.

Go care for your cats.

My legacy lives on!

MY FATHER MY MOTHER MY HERO

 Ava Helmer <AVA.HELMER@gmail.com>   10/29/19
to Gen

Wow. Out of all the insane things that have happened this week (getting herpes, you giving birth to kittens) I think the phone call I just had with my parents takes the cake????

I don't know what I expected but it certainly wasn't this:

*phone rings and rings and rings . . . *

MOM: Hello??
AVA: Where have you been?!
MOM: We went to the movies! Have you seen—
AVA: I haven't seen any movies!
MOM: Any? Now that can't be true—

AVA: Is Dad there?
MOM: You know, I think I lost him at the theater—
DAD: Is that my favorite daughter?
MOM: Oh! I found him!
DAD: I didn't know I was missing!

parents laugh together, still happy and in love

AVA: I have some bad news.
DAD: Uh-oh.
MOM: Are you pregnant?
AVA: No. That would be less permanent.
DAD: Oh, no. You got a tattoo, didn't you?
MOM: Ava! We've talked about this! You said you wouldn't get one until we both die!
AVA: I didn't get a tattoo!
AVA: I got herpes.

long, deafening silence

AVA: Hello?
DAD: Hello.
MOM: Sorry. Are you sure? You've been to a doctor?
AVA: I went yesterday. They have to get the blood work back but the doctor said it was definitely genital herpes.
DAD: Well without the blood work—
AVA: I HAVE HERPES, DAD! OKAY! I HAVE HERPES!
DAD: But without—
MOM: She has herpes, Ken!
DAD: Okay, okay.
MOM: How are you doing? Do you want me to come out there?

AVA: Why? To yell at me for being a stupid slut?

MOM: Ava, no. You're not a slut!

DAD: We don't know that for sure—

MOM: KEN!

DAD: I'm just saying! We don't know what she's been up to. I'm not mad.

MOM: Do you know how you . . . uh . . . got it?

DAD: I'm assuming from sex.

MOM: KEN!

AVA: I don't know. It could have been dormant for years.

MOM: I bet Ben gave it to you. He looks like he's been around the block a few times.

DAD: What about that Dutch guy? They're real wild and loose over there.

AVA: I don't know who gave me herpes, I just know that I have it and my life is over.

MOM: Aw, honey. Your life isn't over.

DAD: I know a guy at the club who has had HIV for at least twenty years. Really good tennis player—

MOM: She doesn't have HIV. Do you?

AVA: Who knows!

loud sobs from one end of the phone

MOM: Sssh. It's okay. I know this is scary but it's just like a cold sore. It's not dangerous.

AVA: It's disgusting!

MOM: How bad is it? Are you in pain?

AVA: Yes.

DAD: Have you taken something? You should take something.

AVA: Are you mad at me?

MOM: Why would we be mad at you? This is life. Life happens!

increased sobbing

CAN YOU BELIEVE THAT?

Life happens????

I thought they would be FURIOUS! And ashamed and disappointed. I mean they probably are all of those things on some level but they're not showing it. At least not to me.

My mom kept offering to come out "just to visit," i.e. "make sure you don't off yourself" but I told her I'd be okay. I think telling them was my biggest fear about this whole thing. (Other than, you know, never being able to have a romantic relationship ever again.)

I feel a crazy sense of relief. If only my vagina would stop burning!

A

Wed, Oct 30, 8:37 AM
KEN AND RUTH FOR THE WIN!
Man, I love those guys!
Ha! Me too.
I woke up to like five links about herpes from my dad.

What about herpes??

Oh, you know. How prevalent it is.
The best medications. And then one
heartwarming story about how a middle-
age divorcée reclaimed her life after
contracting the disease.

Aww! I wanna read that one! I love when
older women reclaim their lives!

She reclaimed it by finding Jesus. I don't
think my dad read the full article.

Fuck. Never mind.

I'm glad you're feeling better!

I WAS feeling better.

Uh-oh. What now? The clap?

I forgot I have to tell every guy I've ever
been with that I have herpes!

That's not true!

You just have to work backwards until
you find the guy that gave YOU herpes.

Should we make bets?

No.

I vote Marcos.

I never slept with Marcos!

YOU slept with Marcos!

Oh, right! That was a crazy summer!

SPOOKY SCARY

 Gen Goldman <GEN.GOLDMAN@gmail.com> 10/30/19
to Ava

. . . Hey! Wanna rewatch all of *30 Rock* at the same time?

I can't believe Halloween is in four days and I don't even have my costumes! I think I'm going to go with some sort of theme this year so my costume changes make more sense to everyone. Maybe something political? Or famous cats throughout history!

Tabby and her babies are doing great! I'm so glad I invited a homeless man into my home to take care of them. Lyle/Beulah managed to delay meeting Beau IRL by saying "her" cat had kittens so "she" needs to stay home and take care of them. Beau apparently found this excuse heartwarming and "sexy as all hell." EEP! So gross.

The only problem in this brilliant move is Lyle forgot to tell me about it so I bounded into work today shouting about my brand-new kittens. Beau looked at me funny before drawling, "What a coincidence. My lady's cat just had kittens too."

I swear to Evan Rachel Wood (aka God), I thought I was caught. But then I realized he GENUINELY THOUGHT it was a coincidence. Bless that man and his simple heart. The only sizeable downside is I now can't show anyone at the office my grandchildren because Lyle already sent Beau photos. Although maybe he wouldn't even notice . . . If you've seen one cat you've seen them all. JUST KIDDING! Paul, James and Eartha are unique unicorns who are too good for this earth(a).

Do you think they are too young to wear costumes? Only reply if your answer is no. I refuse to listen to reason on this subject!

GEN, the mad cat-ter

Re: SPOOKY SCARY!

 Ava Helmer <AVA.HELMER@gmail.com>   10/30/19
to Gen

That's it. I am putting my foot down. Beulah has to break up with Beau. It's the only ethical option. This poor man needs to get on Match.com. Or maybe you can give him one of the cats! He is clearly very lonely.

I almost did a very bad thing at work today but then Dana stopped me. He must have overheard my phone call with my parents last night, specifically when I was shouting, "I HAVE HERPES." So when I made a beeline towards Ben's desk he intercepted me. He steered me into the stairwell and advised I "wait until the weekend" to discuss . . . you know.

This was a very reasonable and smart suggestion. So, naturally, I immediately started crying. Why can't I control my crying? I see all these other people, just walking around, harboring who knows what, and they're not crying! Should I stop drinking so much water??

After getting snot on Dana's new bomber jacket, we decided I would show up unannounced at his place this weekend. Dana thinks Ben would do anything to avoid a face-to-face confrontation if he knows it's coming. Looks like we're going to have ourselves an old-fashioned stakeout! Unless he's already home.

I support any and all human costumes but I will report you to PETA if you try to stuff those little guys into a bodysuit.

Still crying a little!

Ava

P.S. My dad won't stop sending me articles about herpes. I don't want to imagine what his search history looks like right now.

6:13 PM

I have good news and bad news.

Pass.

I can't take any more bad news.

Okay, I'll start with the good news.

You're not respecting my boundaries . . .

Beau is preschool BFFs with the mayor's chief of staff!

Is that the good news or the bad news?

Good! He has an in to the heart of the city!

And he's going to set me up with an interview to discuss Open All Doors.

That's great!!!

What a change of heart!

Exactly! Which leads me to the bad news . . .

Beulah and Beau can't break up.

At least not anytime in the near future.

GEN!

Why is this so bad??? Who am I hurting????

Beau is happier than ever! And Beulah is really coming into her own as a fictional character.

Oh please! You're only doing this for your own personal gain.

Well, yeah! That part was obvious!

I have a family to feed after all!

Fancy Feast doesn't buy itself!

I'm signing off from this conversation in an effort to focus on self-care.

We'll miss you!

WHAT IS THE OPPOSITE OF MERCURY IN RETROGRADE

 Gen Goldman <GEN.GOLDMAN@gmail.com> 10/31/19

to Ava

Because things are really coming up Goldman! All of the children are happy and healthy, Beau has had a personality transplant and Coralee just invited me to a haunted house party tomorrow night. Her boyfriend's motorcycle club is throwing it as some fund-raiser. For what exactly? I think just another party? Who cares! Time is a flat circle! And I love haunted houses!

I'm going to have to up my costume game given the circumstances of meeting the boy-toy. Is RuPaul too on the nose? I won't have done my job if I don't make most of the bikers uncomfortable. Not to get ahead of myself but this is pretty much an invitation to a threesome, right? Like how else could this possibly end? Maybe in unjust police violence but that's always on the table down here (and everywhere).

Oh! My dad called yesterday. He must have remembered he has two daughters and not just the one. I didn't answer. If you don't care enough to leave a message, I'm not obligated to call back. Them's the rules!

How you doing? I don't want to jinx it but part of me thought you would have flown home or checked yourself into an institution by now (not that you can't still do that). I'm very proud of how well you appear to be holding it together. Maybe the herpes has made you stronger???? It could be like your spider bite! (That's a reference to Spider-Man. I know your superhero knowledge is a bit lacking. Still reeling about you thinking Chris Pine was Captain America in *Wonder Woman*. . . .)

I have to say this Dana guy seems to be a good Gen understudy. Maybe he's my soul mate. OR maybe he's YOUR soul mate. I can't believe you haven't at least kissed yet! I kiss all of my roommates at least once. Lyle and I kissed on his second night here! It was way too wet and platonic.

YOU GUYS SHOULD DO A COUPLE'S COSTUME! I CAN HELP!

I am very good at costumes and also having sex with couples!

Gen

P.S. If you can't tell, it's 9:25 and I'm already on my third cup of coffee. I also ate some Skittles. When was the last time you had Skittles? TASTE THE RAINBOW*

*This email was not sponsored by Skittles. I swear.

Re: WHAT IS THE OPPOSITE OF MERCURY IN RETROGRADE

Ava Helmer <AVA.HELMER@gmail.com>   10/31/19
to Gen

I don't want to sound like an "old fart" here, but there is the SLIGHTEST of possibilities that you have just been invited to a party and not to a costumed threesome. And you can't accuse me of being a naive prude anymore because I'm the only one in this friendship with an incurable STI! I don't think it's given me superpowers but it's definitely given me street cred, right? RIGHT????

You never told me you kissed Lyle!! How did that even happen? And why is he still living with you???

You're joking about me and Dana? I think the possibility of him "like-liking" me is pretty much ZERO. Do you know how difficult I am to live with? I created chore charts! CHORE CHARTS! No one likes those! I didn't even like myself while I made them! I think he is just a really good guy who (luckily) finds my misery amusing and *maybe* a bit endearing. There is no way he sees me as anything other than an inept little sister (even though I'm two months older). If I tried to start anything, he would laugh in my face. Not to mention my venereal disease! If there was ever a chance for something more, my open sores have certainly closed that door. Why would you even suggest such a thing? It's ridiculous!

I have to go. Halona wants every intern to present a possible field piece and I have to go figure out if I have any interests or ambitions left. I also have to go get someone's suitcase they "forgot" at JFK. Which means I have to take a taxi all the way to JFK to pick up what I can only assume is a bomb! Why else would you "forget" your suitcase? Unless you are so fucking rich you can lose a bunch of clothes and not notice? Except they did notice because they are sending me to get it . . .

In case you couldn't tell, I'm in a bad mood. I blame the absence of Skittles.

4:12 PM
Methinks thou dost protest too much!
Re: Dana!

4:44 PM
Oh, no!
Was the suitcase a bomb?!

4:57 PM
I don't know who to sue about this but I know I'm going to sue someone!

5:16 PM

Crisis averted! It was not a bomb!

I repeat, the suitcase was not a bomb!

Whew! I was about to get your lawyer of a dad on the horn!

Sorry for the scare. I was fighting with TSA.

Oooo! I love fighting with TSA!

Did they try to give you an unnecessary body search?

For picking up a suitcase?

They'll use any excuse to search you! Those perverts!

My body did not get searched. But my dignity was destroyed.

Apparently you need "proper ID" to claim an abandoned item.

Something no one told me.

How did you get the bag??

I cried.

Ah! The power of a woman's tears!

That's what the guy said!

Fri, Nov 1, 7:13 AM

HAPPY HALLOWEEN!!!!!

I don't think you have ever been up this early before.

Also, it's not Halloween.

It's Halloween WEEKEND!

IT'S THE SAME THING, HEATHEN!

I hate Halloween.

I find costumes stressful and annoying.

Are you trying to break up with me???

Because it's working.

I don't want to get out of bed.

Uh-oh!

What's going on?

Depression. Anxiety. A general malaise.

Hello darkness my old friendddddddd

There is also painful throbbing in my genitals.

Fuck! Are the meds not working?

It takes like 7 to 10 days.

Just long enough to fully hate yourself.

That can't be true!

You already hated yourself!

No! I was on the upswing!

And now I'm in the sewer system with that scary clown.

Which scary clown?

You know which one.

I know but do YOU?

IT!

You mean Pennywise?

Is this payback for my Halloween comment? Or do you actually want me to kill myself?

When is your next therapy appointment?

I don't know. She's been out of town.

What?! Therapists can't go out of town!

Anyone can go out of town. Unless you're released on bail.

Go eat some breakfast, grouchy.

Fine.

I wish I was the kind of depressive who lost their appetite.

- Why not just wish you weren't a depressive?
- STOP PUTTING YOUR UNREALISTIC STANDARDS ON ME AND MY SON
- Maybe have some coffee too.

HALLOWEEN IS RUINED

Gen Goldman <GEN.GOLDMAN@gmail.com> 11/2/19
to Ava

I can't believe I even have the emotional energy to write this right now. It must be the rage coursing through my body. Where do I begin?! I suppose with the beginning of time and internalized misogyny? Actually, fuck it. I don't care enough to give a crash course on why the patriarchy has ruined yet another young life.

The most fucked-up part of all this is how incredible my costume was. Turns out, Lyle Rainbow is quite the seamster and he managed to make me a full Babadook costume while I was at work. (We all know the B in LGBT stands for Babadook.) I wanted to invite him to the party but I was too embarrassed to tell him I was going to a biker fund-raiser. So we parted ways around 8PM so he could go meet up with his beach friends and I could lose all of my dignity for the sake of a Southern threesome.

In typical Coralee fashion, she didn't even text me the address until I was already on my way there (one of

Phyllis's kids was going and I snagged the info from him earlier. Southern people might be racist and homophobic but they are very polite.)

It took me a full hour of scaring the shit out of people before I found her. Turns out, the Babadook is not as popular as we think. At least not when it's homemade and female. Up to three different members of the motorcycle club asked if I was at the wrong party. I don't think they meant this as an insult. I think they were genuinely concerned on my behalf.

I finally spotted Coralee in the middle of a keg stand. Girl after my own heart. Or so I thought. She was dressed as slutty Dorothy, which I think we can all agree is a timeless costume. A loud squeal emanated from her tiny body as she rushed to me and buried her head in my chest. She then kissed me RIGHT ON THE LIPS, causing her to get black Babadook lip stain all over her angelic face. Now, you know me, and I love a spontaneous makeout session, but this seemed a little too brazen even for old Gen. Her very hetero and probably conservative boyfriend was RIGHT there. I'm not here to steal your girl. I'm here to *share* your girl. Ya know?

After sticking her tiny tongue in my mouth (she has the tiniest tongue of anyone I have ever tongued), she dragged me over to meet Deacon Mason, who is much shorter in real life. He's barely five ten. But built like a wrestler with a steroid addiction. I went to shake his hand, man to man, but he swooped down and kissed my cheek instead.

DEACON MASON: "So nice to meet the little lady's friend from the big city!"

What big city?? Los Angeles? Boston? Jacksonville? Also, FRIEND?? I've seen more of your little lady than you have, sir. Because I like to GET IN THERE, not just visit!

This should have been the first tip-off that things were not going to go my way. But I had already chugged some brewskies with my new boys so I was feeling less skeptical. Coralee pulled me and Deacon, who was wearing a vintage Dan Marino jersey as a costume, into a gazebo so we could "get to know each other better." This was a mistake. I should never try to "get to know" anyone.

Another BIG mistake was asking them how they met. Apparently, neither could remember? It was "sometime" "at night" and she looked "good" so they had to "you know" and now they are "so happy, right baby?" Straight people terrify me.

The conversation eventually turned to my history with Coralee and that's where things get f-ed. I'm pretty drunk so I sort of mimic Deacon's story and say things like "we met at night" and "she looked good." His good natured dough-y face was now turning into one of confusion. I was talking about his girlfriend as an object of sexual desire and it fucking rocked his world. He literally interrupted me to ask—

"Wait. Are you gay?"

As if my Babadook costume didn't speak for itself! He didn't understand the reference so I explained I preferred the word *queer.* Or *bi.* In honor of my costume. He, again, didn't understand this reference and looked shocked.

"I don't think I've ever met a gay girl in real life."

I replied: HAHAHAHAHAHAHAHAHAHAHA! You're dating one!

Now, in retrospect, I should not have said this for a variety of reasons.

1) I have no right to define another person's sexuality even if I have had sex with that person.

2) He clearly had no idea that Coralee was anything other than pin straight.

I guess it was only two big reasons but still! I fucked up. I do not think that excused what happened next, which was a complete denial of Coralee's and my shared history.

Before Deacon Mason could fully (if ever) comprehend my comment, Coralee swooped in and said that I had a bit of a crush on her but it had never led to anything other than a few public makeouts for the benefit of the mostly male GOTCHA clientele. "Who doesn't like watching a few girls kiss, babydoll?"

Yes, she calls Deacon Mason "babydoll." Deacon seemed to think for a minute, although there is no way to know for sure what is going on in there, before grumbling, "Don't seem fair that two girls were kissing and I didn't get to see it."

DON'T SEEM FAIR, SIR?! That two women are able to have sexual experiences for the sake of themselves and not the male gaze!

I was unable to get this important point out before Coralee's tiny tongue was back in my mouth! But this time I knew it had nothing to do with me. I was a sex toy to her. Not a person. So I pushed her off and cursed them both in the Babadook's native language! (Which basically amounts to loud, guttural screams.) I ran from the gazebo and somehow found my way home without losing my top hat.

I went to bed crying while also eating nachos.

I hate men. I hate Coralee. And I hate Florida.

MY HEART IS NOT A PLAYGROUND! GO PLAY SOMEWHERE ELSE! YOU DUMB DICK!

G

4:25 PM

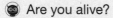 Are you alive?

5:12 PM

I guess.

Did you see my email?

I sorta skimmed it. Haven't really done much today.

. . .

If I only sorta skimmed your emails you would fly to Florida and strangle me.

I guess I don't really see what the big deal is.

Wow.

You knew she was straight. It's not like she was gonna come out to her alpha boyfriend in front of all his friends.

I really hope this is the herpes talking . . .

That's not funny.

Jesus.

Let me know if you can ever bother yourself enough to read it.

UNACCEPTABLE BEHAVIOR

 Gen Goldman <GEN.GOLDMAN@gmail.com>   11/4/19

to Ava

Look, I get it. You have herpes and your whole life is falling apart. But I have a life too and it is also falling apart. I mean, not really, but I did have a horrible Halloween weekend. Alright maybe not the *whole* weekend but Friday was awful and I needed my best friend and you WERE NOT THERE. That is fucked up.

But, in the spirit of my favorite holiday, I will preemptively forgive you. Mostly because I now live in the middle of nowhere and can't afford to lose one more iota of my social life. Texting you counts as part of my social life, right?

Luckily for both of us, I had Lyle Rainbow to lick my wounds. We went trick-or-treating together, mostly to freak people out. Tabby refused to wear her Princess Leia costume so we had to leave her and the babies at home. I got five different packages of Skittles* so it was a pretty great night!

I also reached out to Alex who was surprisingly empathetic about the situation. (You can't be mad at me for reaching out! You left me NO choice.) He made me realize I should pity Coralee. She's too afraid to be herself. That's her problem, not mine. He might come visit. I don't know!

HAVE YOU LEFT YOUR BED? WHERE IS DANA?

If you don't answer me soon I will have no choice but to call your parents, young lady.

G

*Still not sponsored by Skittles but remaining hopeful.

P.S. I have my interview with the mayor's COS today. Wish me luck, patience and the ability to not get kicked out of City Hall.

3:45 PM

If I was a dog my tail would be between my legs in shame.

You would be such a cute dog.

I'm sorry, Gen. I really spiraled this weekend.

It's okay. I only hold grudges against men.

I did a bad thing . . .

I know! You ignored me all weekend!

Right. I did two bad things.

Ooooo do tell.

Too long to text.

Is it safe to say you are still alive or are these texts from the afterlife?

I wish I was dead.

Or in some sort of simulation.

Oh, we are definitely in a simulation.

The real question is, what kind!

I hope it's the kind with a reset button.

Based on my extensive research, that is highly unlikely.

Fuck.

I WILL NOT BE IGNORED

 Ava Helmer <AVA.HELMER@gmail.com>   11/4/19

to Gen

I wish I was just making a *Fatal Attraction* reference and not actually quoting one of the many things I

screamed this weekend. My throat is actually sore.
How do people on reality TV scream at each other so
much? They must take vocal training.

Our stakeout started out really well. Dana and I went
and got donuts and coffee (well, cronuts and lattes)
before hiding behind a van on Ben's block. Did I wish
we had a car to wait in? Absolutely! Did I refuse to sit
on the sidewalk the entire time because of the germs?
You betcha! So now my ego *and* my legs are extremely
sore.

After about an hour of shitting on Ben's taste in
comedy we realized we had never checked to see if
he was home. So Dana gave me a pep talk before
sending me across the street and up the stairs. Here
are highlights from said talk:

1) In the grand scheme of life, Ben does not matter. He
was a part of my story but will not be a part of my future.

2) He does not have any right to shame me for having
herpes. We had consensual sex and I was unaware of
my condition at the time. I am not at fault at all and am
going above and beyond to tell him in person.

3) Try to stay calm, cool and collected. He is not worth
my emotional energy.

4) Look him right in the eye. It's harder to challenge
someone when they are looking you right in the eye.

Spoiler alert: the moment I walked across the street his
words of wisdom evaporated and I was driven by pure

animal instinct. In a bad way. Animals are not great at rationally resolving conflict.

I was able to follow an elderly lady into the building so I didn't have to buzz up, allowing for a "sneak attack." Just as I was bracing myself to knock, the door swung open. INTO MY FACE. Yes, he hit me with the door. Because when it rains, it pours public humiliation and physical agony.

I'm not the best at picking up on social cues, but I think it was rather obvious Ben was NOT happy to see me. Mostly because he saw me and said, "Fuck. Why are you here?" I replied: "You just hit me in the face."

Things were not off to a good start.

BEN: "Can we do this later? I'm running late."
A SHALLOW SHELL OF MYSELF: "Can we do WHAT later? You don't even know why I'm here."
BEN: "I can deduce. And I don't have time for either option."
A SHALLOW SHELL OF MYSELF: "Which are . . ."

shockingly long eye roll for a straight guy

BEN: "One: you want to yell at me. Two: you want to get back together and when I say no, you will yell at me."

ARE YOU SERIOUS??? The audacity! I would NEVER assume someone wanted to get back together with me unless they did something incredibly dramatic, like getting my name tattooed on their arm! Even then, I would be like, "Is this a prank?"

A **FURIOUS** SHALLOW SHELL OF MYSELF: "I'm not here to yell at you—"
BEN: "You're yelling right now."
A **FURIOUS** SHALLOW SHELL OF MYSELF: "I have herpes! I came here to tell you I have herpes."

brief pause

BEN: "That sucks. I'm sorry. But I really have to run—"
A **FURIOUS** SHALLOW SHELL OF MYSELF: "What?! I just told you I have herpes! And we've slept together!"
BEN: "I know and that sucks. But this place does not hold reservations if you're later than like five minutes—"
A **FURIOUS** SHALLOW SHELL OF MYSELF: "Aren't you worried *you* might have—Oh, my god. You already know. BECAUSE YOU GAVE IT TO ME!"
BEN: "Keep your voice down. We can talk about it later."
A **FURIOUS** SHALLOW SHELL OF MYSELF: "No! We will talk about this now! Unless you want me to go to the police!"
BEN: "Why would you go to the police?"
A **FURIOUS** SHALLOW SHELL OF MYSELF: "Because you didn't disclose your STI status! That is a sexual crime!"
BEN: "That's only for HIV. I've googled it."
A **FURIOUS** SHALLOW SHELL OF MYSELF: "You've GOOGLED IT! Because you know what you're doing is bad?!"

BEN: "I haven't had an outbreak in years. You might not even have gotten it from me—"

This is when I went into a guttural scream, while Ben took off down the stairs. In case you're worried that I didn't cause enough of a scene, don't be: I followed him. Still screaming. By the time we hit the ground floor, Ben was completely ignoring me. But that didn't stop me from giving him every single piece of my mind! Including my thoughts on his stand-up (sexist, unoriginal, too much setup with too little payoff). My voice must have really carried, since Dana was waiting at the front door to intercept. This did not go over well with Ben, who I now think is a demon sent from hell to test me.

BEN: "Seriously? You brought this guy? Can't we keep our shit between us?"
A SCREAMING LUNATIC NAMED AVA: "He knew! He knew he had herpes and he didn't tell me!"
DANA: "I heard. From across the street."
BEN: "Can we do this later? I'm gonna lose this reservation and I booked it weeks ago—"
A SCREAMING LUNATIC NAMED AVA: "You don't deserve to eat!"

Dana attempts to subdue the lunatic with a calm presence and points of reason. Lunatic ignores this and tries to hit Ben with purse only to fail, having little experience hitting people with over-the-shoulder bags. The straps are never as long as you want them to be.

A SCREAMING LUNATIC NAMED AVA: "This isn't over! You can't just walk away from me!"

Ben walks away while an older couple stares. They're not angry. But they are disappointed.

AND THAT WAS MY SUNDAY!

I wish I could say it was my worst Sunday on record but we both know that isn't even true . . . (RIP junior year vomit pants. I don't miss you.)

This disaster of a morning is obviously not an excuse for ignoring you, but I clearly have not been in a good headspace. I even thought about calling in sick to work today, but I didn't want to make it that easy on Ben. Joke's on me. HE called in sick! What a little sleazeball coward!

I mean it's probably for the best since I usually need a full forty-eight hours to calm down, but STILL. How dare he not show his evil, normal-oily face! (It used to be full oily but I bought him this really nice face wash from Kiehl's when I still thought he was deserving of basic beauty care.)

I want to warn Lacie about him since they are still obviously hanging out, but Dana said he should do it to avoid unnecessary "drama" (aka me being overly dramatic). He has been so levelheaded and rational about this whole thing. Most people would have told me to check myself into a psych ward by now so I would leave them alone. Is it bad if I feel conflicted about telling Lacie? She would be the first person to know about the big H other than my closest friends (2) and family (also 2). Once five people know about something it's pretty much on the tip of going public . . .

PLUS if I know Ben at all (which I maybe don't) they've probably already had (unprotected) sex so what would the point be of exposing myself anyway??

Wow. I'm gonna need you to delete this immediately after reading. I seem awful! And possibly a threat to society.

A

Re: I WILL NOT BE IGNORED

 Gen Goldman <GEN.GOLDMAN@gmail.com>   11/4/19

to Ava

HOLY SHITE! And you know I only use British slang when I'm REALLY pissed!

What a Francesco Schettino! (That's the cruise captain who abandoned ship before his passengers. It's important to get creative when calling someone a coward. You have to really stick it to them.)

On the one hand, Ben's behavior is so deplorable I find myself absolutely and completely SHOOK.

On the second hand, huh? Maybe we should have seen this coming. Not the secret herpes or his obsession with getting to a reservation on time per se, but his general douchiness and disregard for women and probably people in general. I know I've never met the guy in person but I have spent far more time than I will ever admit creeping on his social. And I got to tell ya, those Instagram captions? Clearly the work of a psychopath. He did a #tbt on a WEDNESDAY. Who does he think he is? Obama?

I'm glad he called in sick to work. Normally I don't promote violence . . . Actually that's not true. I think I might actually promote violence a lot. But only when these dickheads really deserve it.

Speaking of dickheads, I had my meeting at the mayor's office just now. I was scheduled to meet with the COS but was handed over to his assistant. Sheila, age unknown but possibly only twelve, refused to answer any of my questions and instead wrote them all down to relay to her boss. WHO I WAS SUPPOSED TO SPEAK TO IN THE FIRST PLACE. I felt like I had shown up on a first date, all dolled up and optimistic, only to find a robot sent in place of my future wife. And not even a cute, charming robot! A robotic robot who is clearly still in the beta presale phase. I don't think Sheila's facial muscles moved once. Even when she was talking! Maybe that's why she looked prepubescent. She could have been fifty-five!

What if this whole journey was leading me to Sheila . . . an undercover, top-secret government robot? Is it obvious I've been watching too much "recommended in sci-fi" on Netflix?

The only good that came from this was Beau's surprising indignation at my mayoral shun. He took it upon himself to call up his old friend and demand an in-person interview unless the chief of staff wants us looking into *his* background instead. Specifically, the summer of 2004. I now have another interview with the COS **and** the MAYOR(!) on Thursday! Say what you will about the ethics of entrapping your coworker with a fictional Facebook account, Beulah has done wonders for Beau's self-esteem. Wonders!

Re: Lacie, I think we both know you need to tell her (or have Dana tell her). I'm sure she won't want to tell anyone either, but if you keep it from her and she does contract it, I don't think you'll be able to live with yourself. You closed the door on an old lady by ACCIDENT two years ago and it kept you up at night for a week! You're a good, moral, responsible person. Herpes can't change that! (Wow, did I just write an ad campaign for herpes?)

Before I go eat Taco Bell with my cats, I want to leave you a few possible ideas I had for what could possibly have happened to the Fernandina Beach mayor's COS in the summer of 2004:

1) Drug trip gone bad that ended in public defecation.

2) Misguided office crush that turned into sexual harassment case.

3) Drug trip gone bad that ended in public fornication.

4) Cried during *The Incredibles* and then lied about it.

5) Alligator murder.

If you think of any other possibilities, PLEASE let me know.

I love you with every fiber of my misandrist being,

G(ournalist)

8:42 PM

What if Beau caught that guy making out with his mom?

Oooo!

I LIKE WHERE YOUR HEAD IS @ GURL

My head is all I have since my body and personality are garbage.

Okay now I don't like where your head is either.

Triple threat/failure.

Tue, Nov 5, 9:17 AM

The prodigal son returns.

I don't think you're using that reference correctly.

Does it not mean "that son of a bitch" is back?

Actually I have no idea. I don't understand the Bible.

I can't believe he had the nerve to show his face here!

Same. But also, it's his job.

Since when are you the reasonable one?

I'm not! I swear!

Oh really???

When was the last time you did something irresponsible?

This isn't about me!

Oh my god. You love to make everything about you . . .

WHAT DID YOU DO?????

It doesn't matter. What are you going to do about Ben?

I'll only tell you if you promise to tell me your thing later.

FINE!!!!!!

You should be a lawyer!

You're about as likable.

😎

I'm going to ignore him.

But I am going to talk to Lacie.

IRL???

I think so. But Dana will be there too to back me up and potentially administer a tranquilizer if she doesn't believe me.

Sounds like a plan!

I have to go uncover whether the mold in the local YMCA is toxic or not.

Isn't all mold toxic???

Probably, yeah.

WHAT DID YOU DO!?

Ava Helmer <AVA.HELMER@gmail.com>   11/5/19
to Gen

Please tell me. I need to not be the "bad" one anymore.

Re: WHAT DID YOU DO!?

Gen Goldman <GEN.GOLDMAN@gmail.com>   11/5/19
to Ava

Hahaha! You're not BAD! What have you done that is morally reprehensible?? Fallen for a guy who pretended to be nice and interested in you? Yelled at said guy when he turned out not to be so nice? Stood up for yourself and your body in a time of peril???

Don't come at me with that herpes is "bad" shit. It's a disease and like any other disease there is nothing moral or immoral about it! OKAY, SWEETIE????

I think the same applies for my "transgression." There is nothing WRONG with it but it may or may not be TABOO. Which is stupid and just a product of our dumb society. Human behavior is constantly evolving and all the things/acts deemed "unsightly" now will probably be the norm in like two hundred years if there is still a planet.

Anyway, I hooked up with the bartender at GOTCHA last night in the break room. I think he thinks my name is Gwen. Felt like role-playing!

How's the ol' Big Apple? Seen any celebs?

G

3:13 PM

You hooked up with a bartender in public???

Who is this?

Gen! Anyone could have walked in!

I know! That's half the fun!

Did you even like the guy?

I liked him enough for 1:15AM on a Tuesday morning!

This is making me sad.

Why???

I was bored and then I wasn't.

I took my life into my own hands! That's feminism.

. . .

I don't know what to say.

No need to say anything

That's what journaling is for!

Isn't this dangerous??? He's basically a complete stranger!

No he's not! I go to GOTCHA all the time.

And Lyle was there.

In the room with you???

HA! No. Even Lyle has limits.

He was at the bar.

So he couldn't exactly protect you.

No one protected you from Ben.

That's different!

How?

Because you "knew" him?

Most violence occurs in relationships!

Just like how most car accidents happen a mile from your home.

Fuck you and your twisted statistics.

It feels good to win.

GIRL POWER!

 Ava Helmer <AVA.HELMER@gmail.com>   11/6/19
to Gen

Or whatever the politically correct term is today. I think I just had the most successful meeting of our generation. But I'm getting ahead of myself. We all know how important it is to set the scene.

It was a mild day by November New York standards, which meant I was still freezing my ass off. (I don't think my delicate skin can handle anything outside of the 75- to 85-degree range. Why did I move here?)

Dana and I came in early (like 6AM early) to help a couple of the other interns build this ridiculous set for tonight's show. Apparently the floor will represent lobbyists and needs to look like lava? I don't know.

They should have hired someone who actually knows what lava looks like . . . Or, at the very least, knows how to use a glue gun.

By 8AM we were all pretty loopy and bonding over the misery of not being recognized for our certain genius. Apparently, every single one of us is an unrecognized comedic genius. What are the odds? We finished up around one and then were allowed to take a long lunch as payment for our extra hard work. (Not a paid lunch! Just a regular lunch with some extra padding for a nap.)

After a bit of strategic planning on my part, Dana, Lacie and I separated from the group to try out this new taco place a few blocks over. Everyone else went for pizza because I'm now in N.Y. and not L.A. I had to really push the carne asada even though I don't eat meat . . .

Regardless of my less-than-truthful tactics, I finally had Lacie alone! Well, alone plus Dana, which honestly feels like the same as being alone. In a good way! I think I might be in love with Dana. More on that later . . .

The taco place was empty because the food ended up being disgusting but it made us feel like we were alone. Which is a hard thing to accomplish in N.Y. I could tell Lacie was a bit uncomfortable so I tried to get to the point as soon as possible to avoid any awkward silences. (You know how much I hate those. I'd rather babble for hours than be alone with my own thoughts in the company of others.) I did my best to be direct and succinct.

ME: "I have herpes."
LACIE: "Oh . . . okay."

one of those long pauses I hate

DANA: "Ben gave Ava herpes."
LACIE: "OH."
BEN: "That's why she's telling you."
LACIE: "OHHH . . . What? I've never had sex with Ben."
AVA/DANA: "You haven't?!"
LACIE: "Ew. No. I would never sleep with that guy. No offense."

offense taken

ME: "But I thought—"
LACIE: "I mean . . . He *tried* to sleep with me. And we hung out a couple times. But we never did anything that would lead to me getting . . . you know."
AVA: "So you did do some stuff???"
LACIE: "I mean . . . define stuff."
AVA: "YOU define stuff!"
DANA: "I don't think we need to get into specifics. Ava just wanted to warn you to use protection in case you guys were sleeping together."
LACIE: "You didn't use protection?"
AVA: "You can get it either way. I wanted to warn you because he didn't tell me he had it and if you're going to put yourself at risk you deserve to know that you are making that decision and not have someone else make it for you."

another long pause that made my skin itch

LACIE: "That's actually really sweet of you."

AVA: "Yeah. Of course."

LACIE: "So he didn't tell you he had it?"

AVA: "No."

LACIE: "That's fucked up. He should get fired."

AVA: "I don't think you can fire someone for having an STI."

LACIE: "Yeah . . . But you *can* fire someone for sleeping with the intern."

And that's where the conversation really took off. It never occurred to me that Ben could get in trouble over our relationship since he was so obvious about it. Everyone knew. Like even the cleaning staff. One time I forgot my sweater in the kitchen and they left it on his desk. It doesn't get more in-your-face than that!

But . . . just because it's an open secret doesn't mean it's not against the rules. Especially considering the circumstances. (Him not revealing his herpes status and then dumping me. Normally you'd think I'd at least get to do the dumping, but no! Completely powerless!) Lacie thinks if I bring a complaint against Ben to HR, there is no way they could ignore it. Especially considering it's a female-run show (that happens to be run by a woman who hates women but most people don't know that).

I don't know what to do. I obviously want Ben gone but I also don't want to be labeled "vindictive herpes girl." It would be different if he forced himself on me in some way but I did consent to everything (other than herpes exposure but no relationship is perfect!).

I think the part that is hardest about this whole thing is feeling like there is this huge part of me I can't talk about anymore. I am not good at keeping things to myself. I once spent fifteen minutes talking to a cashier about my irrational fear of tuberculosis because it's mentioned in every single medication commercial so it must be a huge threat to everyday Americans. (We actually really hit it off. I still follow her on Instagram.)

But NOW I can never tell people what I'm worrying about or if open sores on my vulva are causing me discomfort. I have to walk around carrying this secret shame, hating myself for not demanding STD paperwork before taking off my clothes for what will probably end up being the last time.

How can I be a writer if I can't even write about myself??? Maybe I should switch to fantasy. Or superheroes. Those seem to be really popular and by-the-book. I bet I could do that?

Anyway, my hands are tired from typing. And my soul is tired from being alive.

To reiterate:

Option A: I try to get Ben fired.
Option B: I write superhero movies under a moniker?

Let me know your thoughts,

A

Re: GIRL POWER!

 Gen Goldman <GEN.GOLDMAN@gmail.com>   11/6/19

to Ava

Sweetest Ava,

I don't know where to begin. Have you ever even met
someone with tuberculosis? Or have you just seen it in
the movies and on TV commercials? I'm starting to
think the whole disease was eradicated years ago
and the government is just using it as a fear tactic . . .
Is this my next exposé? Probably not.

Next topic: Lacie seems like a real pleasure (sort of).
That said, I'm very proud of you for putting your fears
aside and telling her the truth about that mofo. Part of
me thinks they did sleep together and she's just trying
to save face . . . Why do women feel the need to deny
their sexual life/appetite to protect their "reputation?"
Should that be my next exposé? Probably.

You're in love with Dana??? I can't say I'm shocked.
But I'm peeved I never got the "more on this later" as
promised. You can't leave me hanging like this! Can't
you see I'm starved for content? I'm a print journalist! I
can't even afford Hulu *with* commercials.

And now for what you think was the main topic of
discussion but actually isn't . . . (More on that later. And
I WILL deliver unlike some people.) . . . Should you try
to get Ben fired? I am very conflicted because on the
one hand, I think all men should be fired. And on

the other, this is a decision you have to make entirely for yourself. Two or three years ago, I would have been screaming from the rooftops to "kill them all" but I've seen what this kind of accusation can do to the victim and it's not pretty. Ideally we should live in a world where women can report something bad without THEIR character being called into question. Instead, the moment a woman complains, the entire situation is somehow their fault. And I don't want you to have to face that kind of scrutiny when you're not even sure you want to take action in the first place. This might be one of the awful circumstances where the negatives don't outweigh the positives. Although I am more than willing to send him threatening letters until he resigns in disgrace?? Just let me know! Lyle has a hookup at the post office. (Because he hooked up with someone at the post office.)

THE BIG FINALE! The "more on this later" we have all been waiting for . . .

Why do you think you have to keep your condition a secret? You're an open book, Ava, and nothing will break you more than trying to keep a few key pages to yourself. Might I suggest radical honesty instead? I can't reiterate this enough: the ONLY reason STDs are stigmatized is because WE (society) choose to stigmatize them. You could change the narrative! You could be the face of herpes! Think about how empowering that would be for all the other young people who have it!

If you're not quite ready to have your flawless skin on a billboard, you don't have to go public but you *can* go private. As in IRL but not online. You don't need to hide this part of yourself from anyone you don't want to. You already told your parents! No one else will take it as hard! And from what I've heard, they don't even seem to care that much. It's just given Ken something new to google. Remember last summer when he wouldn't stop sending us articles about the benefits of eating raw? He doesn't even eat raw! What a silly guy! Love him.

I look forward to hearing your thoughts on my thoughts,

G

Thu, Nov 7, 10:27 AM

I can't just go around telling people I have herpes!

Why not?

Because! It will make people uncomfortable!

So?

I'm not telling you to sing it from the rooftops, but if you feel like talking about it you should.

I don't want to talk about it.

🙄

You really think that if someone happens to catch me crying in public and asks "what's wrong" I should reply "i'm upset because I have herpes"??????

I mean you're already crying in public. . . .

What else is there to lose?

You're insane.

Maybe!

Okay, off to meet the mayor!

Good luck!

Luck is what happens when preparation meets opportunity.

Have you prepared?

Nope!

Gonna wing it!

2:13 PM

What happened with Dana???

What happened with the mayor???

Touche.

Email to follow.

Same.

SMALL GOVERNMENT (SMALLER MEN)

 Gen Goldman <GEN.GOLDMAN@gmail.com>   11/7/19
to Ava

I don't know why people continue to shock me. I read the news. I WRITE the news. Humans are deplorable. I understand this concept on a macro level, but each time I meet someone new I think, "Well, this person won't be a rotting piece of human garbage, surely!" And then I meet them and they stink worse than the Paris Sewer System. (I have obviously never smelled the Paris Sewer System but you talk about it all the time because of that one family vacation. So I think it works as a reference.) I'm comparing humans to shit. They stink like shit.

I probably should have seen this coming since the current mayor's predecessor was arrested for domestic violence BEFORE winning the election. So it's obviously a VERY LOW BAR to lead this city into ruin.

The meeting was at 11AM so I made sure I showered and everything. Did I go into the office first? No, but I blow-dried my hair to conform to society's misguided ideas of "acceptable" and "hygienic." I was putting in at least 95 percent. I even showed up two minutes early! Despite being the single mother of multiple newborn kittens! (Lyle is more like a fun uncle than a spouse.)

I then had to wait for forty-five minutes in a HALLWAY because they don't have a waiting room. They claimed budget restrictions. I claim power move. If I wasn't already used to crouching from being a crust punk that one month in Portland, I would have been too tired to grill an elected official about gay rights. (JOKE'S ON YOU! I'm NEVER too tired to talk about gay rights!)

They finally opened up the mahogany doors and ushered me inside. Parker, Beau's buddy from the mystery summer in 2004 and the mayor's chief of staff, immediately told me the mayor was running behind and I could only have a few minutes of his time. As a courtesy.

DOES NO ONE APPRECIATE THE FREE PRESS
ANYMORE???! (Don't answer that.)

Since I only had a "few moments" I got right down to
the nitty gritty. Here is the official transcript:

Gen Goldman, Ace Reporter: "Do you think queer
people should be denied basic human rights such as
food and shelter due to their sexual orientation?"

Parker Something, Political Minion: "Whoa! I thought
this was a light profile on the mayor. You know. A fluff
piece."

Gen Goldman, Ace Reporter: "Why would you
think that? Sir, please answer the question. Do
you think queer people should be denied basic human
rights such as food and shelter due to their sexual
orientation?"

Mayor, Moron: "I'm not going to answer that on the
record."

Gen Goldman, Ace Reporter: "But off the record you
think queer people should be denied basic human
rights such as food and shelter due to their sexual
orientation?"

Parker Something, Political Minion: "Do you have any
other questions?"

Gen Goldman, Ace Reporter: "Should Open All Doors
continue its discriminatory policy when it claims to be a
safe haven for those in need?"

Mayor, Moron: "Well . . . uh, private institutions have the right—"

Gen Goldman, Ace Reporter: "Open All Doors files its taxes as a public charity."

Mayor, Moron: "They do? I mean, yes, they do. But still. Religious organizations have the right to operate under their own laws and edicts*."

*Please note the Mayor, Moron mispronounced edicts as ED-icts.

Gen Goldman, Ace Reporter: "Don't you think the city has a responsibly to take care of its citizens?"

Mayor, Moron: "Uh . . . yes?"

Gen Goldman, Ace Reporter: "So you would agree that Fernandina Beach has an obligation to provide resources for homeless youth who are being turned away from shelters for their sexual identity?"

Parker Something, Political Minion: "Objection."

Gen Goldman, Ace Reporter: "You can't just shout objection. This isn't a courtroom. It's an interview."

I got ushered out pretty quickly after that. I know what you're thinking. I should have been diplomatic. I should have beaten around the bush before going after him with the hard-hitting questions, but I was pissed and I knew I wasn't going to be given enough time. Sometimes you just have to catch them off-guard and go for the jugular. Now I just have to convince Grady to let me rip this man to shreds in the article.

Maybe if Beulah sends her first nude, Beau will be in such a good mood, he'll back me up!

Can I borrow a picture of your boobs? It can be tasteful!

Love you, miss you, wish I could kiss you,

G

P.S. If there is an explosion at the Fernandina Beach Town Hall, please be prepared to be my alibi.

Re: SMALL GOVERNMENT (SMALLER MEN)

 Ava Helmer <AVA.HELMER@gmail.com>   11/7/19
to Gen

Genevieve! You can't make threats against the (small) government online! You of all people should know the NSA is tracking that stuff! They could show up at your door and arrest you! Only make threats against the government in person and away from your phone. Jeez! YOU are the one who taught me that.

I'm not even going to bother to lecture you about confronting the mayor. That guy obviously sucks and you are obviously not enjoying Florida. Do you know how I have Ava Meltdowns™? Well, it seems like you might be on the verge of a Gen Explosion™. Maybe take a few (or fifty) deep breaths before talking to Grady about the interview? Or maybe *never* talk to him about it?

But then again, I have a film degree. What the fuck do I know about real life?

I know I promised you info on the whole "Dana situation" but now I sort of feel dumb that I said anything. There is no way he "likes me" likes me. Especially since the infection. Plus I'm pretty sure he only likes lesbians. Or girls who look like lesbians. I shouldn't even think about him that way. Romance is no longer a part of my life. Maybe I'll be better off! I could accomplish great things if I'm not wasting my time worrying if some random dude will text me back.

I can make being an old maid stylish again! (Not that it was ever stylish . . . Or maybe it was? I have retained nothing from history.)

It would all be a lot easier if I didn't LIVE with the guy and have to see him half naked everyday. Normally the male body repulses me. But not Dana's . . .

Oh god. I have to go take a cold shower. And then permanently move into an igloo.

Ava the Nun

P.S. Please don't be mad at me about the whole Gen

Explosion™ thing. I have so little joy in my life and you're like 75 percent of it.

11:45 PM

What's the other 25 percent?

Fri, Nov 8, 8:11 AM

???

WHAT'S THE OTHER 25 percent OF YOUR JOY!!!!???

OH! Right!

Pizza.

Ah. I'll allow it.

Why are you so sure that you're straight if the male body disgusts you?

MOST male bodies.

MOST.

Do female bodies disgust you?

No. But I still don't want to touch them.

You are so strange, little one.

Also, I'm totally fine to threaten Fernandina Beach in writing.

They don't care enough about Florida to use NSA resources down here.

You might be right.

Send N00dz

No. Beau has been through enough.

LOVE AND OTHER (BETTER) DRUGS

 Gen Goldman <GEN.GOLDMAN@gmail.com>   11/8/19

to Ava

So I've been doing some thinking and I think you're being dumb. (Sorry, not sorry. I've also been doing some drinking.) You can't just turn yourself off from romance and relationships because you have the herp! That's insane!

You're the most love-obsessed person I know! You stopped watching *The West Wing* because there "wasn't enough romance." You cry when old people hold hands! Even if it's just because neither of them can walk without support (Oh, god. That is adorable. Fuck.)

YOU LOVE LOVE!

And I for one will not stand here and let you forget it! (Full disclosure, I'm sprawled out on my couch with the whole threesome on top of me. It's crazy how cats just instinctively know how to stay alive! I barely do anything for them and they seem fine. Actually, that was pretty much how it was, growing up in my dysfunctional household, so maybe it's not so shocking after all. We should just let children raise themselves! My worst habits are things I learned directly from my parents. There should be no parents! Just children raising themselves. And cats! So many precious little cats.)

What I'm trying to say is, KISS DANA! And if Dana doesn't want to kiss you, kiss someone else! You can't give up on your dreams and your dreams seem to involve a straight cis man! Even if I can't understand that dream, I continue to support it!

You are an incredible, funny, smart woman with a much bigger butt than people think.

Everyone (except Republicans) deserve happiness. But you deserve it the most.

So instead of folding in on yourself, EXPAND! BLOOM! Have one of those famous Gen Explosions™ but in a good way!

I am here if you need some sort of sensei to guide you. First tip: assume everyone wants to sleep with you and act accordingly.

P.S. Do you think I should text Coralee and tell her off? Yeah! Me too!

Gen

P.P.S I put the P.S. in the wrong place!!! EGG ON MY FACE! Ew. I hate eggs. I might need to puke.

Sat, Nov 9, 9:12 AM

Are you alive? Or did you die from alcohol poisoning and/or bad decisions???

10:36 AM

GEN!!!!!!

You can't send me bonkers emails like that and then not reply!

You agreed to this! I have it in writing!!

11:12 AM

Gen can't come to the phone right now due to a pounding headache and deep-seated personality problems.

Understood. But the specimen (Gen) remains alive?

Affirmative.

Please send my condolences for her behavior and have her reach out to me at her earliest convenience for a full debriefing.

Roger that, captain.

OY.

4:07 PM

Hello from the bowels of hell!

Hello! Is it warm all the way down there?

Scorching.

And every sound reverberates like a jackhammer.

Hmmm might be a good time to accept Jesus into my heart so I don't end up down there.

- Or you could just avoid drinking an entire bottle of Jameson.
- Smart!
- Are you safe at home? Or in some stranger's hotel room?
- I'm at home but are you ever really safe?
- Ah. I'll wait until you've settled a bit more for my full debriefing.
- Dana and I are going to see a movie.
- Give him a hand job!
- Stop.
- Just sit in the back row! No one will know.
- Enjoy hell.

LOOK

 Gen Goldman <GEN.GOLDMAN@gmail.com> 11/9/19
to Ava

We all make mistakes. And I happened to make a few of mine yesterday. BUT I've barely made *any* mistakes since I started living in this penis-shaped state we call Florida so I feel like I was due a few extras.

Where did the night go wrong? I think it's more important to focus on where my LIFE went wrong. You know: treat the whole being instead of the parts. This is very holistic of me.

Let's start at the beginning, shall we?

My parents meet at an AA meeting. Well, my father was at an AA meeting and my mom was just grabbing a free coffee. She found his history of addiction "endearing." And so their fucked-up love affair began.

I am born. My father is no longer attending AA meetings because he is too drunk to drive to them. My mother has taken to martyrdom like a fish to water. I am colicky in order to make my voice known in the world. They almost divorce.

Age five. I refuse to wear a dress to my birthday party. I throw a fit and "ruin everyone's day." A week later, I start wearing that same dress for a month straight and don't take it off. I SET MY OWN GENDER RULES!

Middle school. I hang with the "fast" crowd but mostly make sarcastic comments and worry about my growing attraction to girls. I also discover porn.

High school. I meet you. Pretty chill.

College. Chaos. Confusion. Lots of "drama." Do very well in some classes. Almost flunk out of others. Waste four years in an on-and-off thing with a guy named Alex who doesn't even seem to like me. The only reason I care is because I must make him like me. It's fine. We still talk. I will win eventually, Alex.

Last night. I slept with both Coralee AND her boyfriend, Deacon Mason. Then I had a shit fit and threw a lamp at a wall. You only live once, right?! (Not right. I'm still on the fence about reincarnation until someone proves to me it's *not* possible.)

I'm assuming you want more details because you are so nosy and it's also a really good story.

It all started with one of my famous sassy late-night texts.

GEN: U Up?

I know what you're thinking. Cheesy. Corny. But that's only if I was some fuckboi and we were both stuck in heteronormative hookup culture. Instead, we are two ladies who have a complicated history and a random dude in the picture, making my use of such a "corny" line ironic and creative. (At least I like to think so.)

Coralee must have agreed because she answered me immediately.

CORALEE: Wat u up 2?

Now, part of me wanted to believe she was simply continuing our clever parody but a larger part of me knew this is just how she texts. But who am I to judge! I have some friends I only communicate with in memes! (Hilarious memes but memes nonetheless.)

GEN: Come over.

CORALEE: Come here.

GEN: Where's here?

CORALEE: Deacon's farm.

Yes. Deacon lives on a farm. But we didn't do it on hay or anything. Although his mattress was pretty lumpy so maybe? I honestly didn't see my night going this way because she is such a slow texter and our last interaction wasn't exactly fun and flirty.

BUT . . . I followed my sex drive. And my pioneering spirit. I was also drunk. Thank God for Lyle! He is my own personal Lyft! I mean his name is basically Lyft already!

I got there expecting to walk right into a ménage but instead walked into another redneck party. I had to take like four shots and explain all of my tattoos before FINALLY getting some alone time with the happy couple.

You know me. I like to have fun. I like to see where the moment takes me. I'm a simple leaf blowing in the wind. But, if I'm going to take part in a threesome, I HAVE to be in charge. That's just the way it is if you want to hop on this old train with a friend. I'm the conductor and we're all in for a fun ride.

Deacon and Coralee got on board with this plan pretty quickly (pun intended, as always). So the sex part of the night was fun. Mind blowing? No. But one heck of a good time, ya hear me!

Afterwards is when things got dicey. Deacon went to the bathroom to shower off and Coralee not so politely asked me to take a hike now that my work was over. Was I planning on staying the night with good ol' Tim McGraw and Faith Hill? No. But a girl likes to be asked. Especially when she just orchestrated a flawless threesome. So I lost my temper a little.

GEN: You're seriously throwing me out?
DISCOUNT FAITH HILL: Don't be so dramatic. You make him uncomfortable.
GEN: He didn't seem uncomfortable a minute ago when—
DISCOUNT FAITH HILL: He's my boyfriend, Gen. He can't think I have actual feelings for you.
GEN: Do you have feelings for me? Or am I just a cum dumpster?

Sorry for the language. If you want I can resend a toned down PG-13 version of events. Just let me know! Full disclosure: the only change will be subbing in "semen garbage can" for "cum dumpster."

LOSER TIM MCGRAW: What's that? You two ladies are too damn refined to be talking about beautiful things like cum dumpsters.

Knockoff Tim McGraw cackles to himself.

DISCOUNT FAITH HILL: Don't be silly, darling. Gen was just leaving—

Okay, so this is where I threw a lamp. Would love to point out: I was pretty drunk and I hate when people say *darling*. Especially when it's to someone else and I'm standing right there!

Coralee and her *homosapien* started shouting so I

started shouting back and that's when I was "escorted" away. (Deacon Mason carried me outside while I kicked at the air.) It was quite the evening according to all the cows who watched us struggle.

Am I proud of what happened? Kind of! You never really get to throw lamps without repercussions and this was one of those times. I had to take advantage! These people aren't important to me. That lamp wasn't expensive. It was kismet and now I can cross it off the bucket list. (I don't think that time I threw a few flashlights while camping counts.)

And that was my night! I was able to call a cab to get me home since I can only abuse Lyle's kindness before 3AM. Just another Friday!

I can already hear you yelling at me. Please keep it down. My head hurts.

G

9:13 PM
I'm not yelling.
I'm disappointed.
Yeah yeah.
Are you allowed to say "redneck"???
Isn't that a derogatory term?
I think they reclaimed it.
Seems suspicious.

I think my cats are drunk from whatever's seeping out of my skin.

I really hope that's not scientifically possible.

Sun, Nov 10, 10:13 AM

You have ruined my life.

Not my first time getting this text from a girl . . .

What did I do this time?

You told me Dana was in love with me!

He's not?

NO!!

And I'm humiliated!

Okay, slow down.

I don't think I ever said he was in love with you.

I told you not to give up on love!

. . . By going after Dana! And now I have to move!

I HATE MOVING!

He's kicking you out???

Emotionally!

What happened?

And not what do you think happened. What actually happened?

I'm too embarrassed.

Come on! Embarrassing things happen to you all the time!

This can't be THAT bad!

I have to go. I hear him waking up. I must escape.

From the apartment, right???

Not the world???

AVA!!!

10:25 AM

If I was going to kill myself I would have done it already.

There's my girl!

NOWHERE TO RUN, NOWHERE TO HIDE

 Ava Helmer <AVA.HELMER@gmail.com>   11/10/19

to Gen

Dear Genevieve,

I write this from a slightly damp, smelly coffee shop fifteen blocks from my apartment. But I might as well be back inside my shared apartment around 11:30 last night because I can't get that horrible, awful, mortifying moment out of my head. I need to stop eating so many blueberries. I remember things too clearly.

I wish I could blame what happened on alcohol or drug use but I was stone-cold sober. The only thing to blame is my own stupidity. And you. At least 20 percent of this is your fault for giving me false hope. DON'T TRY TO FIGHT ME ON THAT. I'm already claiming

75 percent of the blame. The missing 5 percent goes to movie theater popcorn, because that always fucks me up. Do they put cocaine in there? Maybe I WAS on drugs?

I didn't start the day with plans of grand romantic gestures. I started the day like I always do lately: sad, depressed and ashamed. If anything, I had doubled down on my decision to be a bitter old maid. But then we went to the movie and my heart started to feel things again. . . .

Romantic comedies should come with a warning: PLEASE BE ADVISED. NONE OF THE FOLLOWING IS BASED IN TRUTH AND NONE OF THE FOLLOWING WILL EVER **EVER** HAPPEN TO YOU.

I wonder how many lives have been ruined by Kate Hudson, Reese Witherspoon and Anne Hathaway. Probably too many to count.

I know. I'm deflecting. But I'm not sure if I have the strength to write down what actually happened. It kept me up all night. It's the only thing I could see when I closed my eyes. It's the only thing I can see now. AND MY EYES ARE OPEN.

Am I being primed to become some sort of religious messiah? Is that why I am being tested like this? Because if that's the case, I'm not interested.

The real trouble started when we were back home and I started to head off to my bedroom.

DANA: You're going to bed already? It's Saturday night!

I mistakenly took this to mean a few different things:

1) Dana loves hanging out with me. He literally can't get enough.

2) Saturday night is clearly a euphemism for something.

Neither of those things proved to be true. I think he just didn't want to go to bed yet and I was the only one around. HINDSIGHT and BASIC SOCIAL SKILLS would have really come in handy here.

Anyway, I had neither so I went and joined him on the couch. We started watching Ali G because he is cool and hip like that and then our legs touched. He did not move his leg away. I immediately misread this as love.

A minute or two later, we both cracked up at the same thing and made eye contact. Then, being the pathetic, moronic, excuse of a human being that I am, I TRIED TO KISS HIM! LIKE LIFE IS SOME FUN PASTTIME I GET TO BE A PART OF!

He dodged. And he dodged HARD. I've always thought it was strange when someone said they got kissed "out of nowhere." Wouldn't you be able to avoid a kiss if you didn't want to be kissed? The answer is yes. Yes, you can. And Dana's not even an athlete.

A normal person would have taken this to mean: HE

DOESN'T WANT TO KISS YOU. But I am so delusional I actually thought, "Maybe I just did that wrong" so I went in AGAIN! He had to block me with his **elbow**! Friends who want to be more than friends don't give each other the elbow!

I am honestly shaking just thinking about it. I could maybe, MAYBE, recover if I had just gone in once. But, no. I went in TWICE. It's just too much shame to handle. I'm at a new low. I spilled tea all over myself on the way to this sticky table and I didn't even bother to try to clean it up. That's who I am now. A tea-covered, herpes-infected, unpaid intern who can't show her face in her own home. I might have a third-degree burn under my bralette. But it's hard to tell because I can only feel emotional pain now.

After Dana gave me the elbow, I jumped up and started rambling.

AVA: Sorry. I'm sorry. I thought. Gen. I'm so sorry—
DANA: Hey, it's okay. It's just not really a good idea.
AVA: Because of the herpes?
DANA: Because we're friends.

Seriously??? Can you think of a more hurtful reason?!!! I even gave him an out! Blame the herpes! It's not personal! I wouldn't want to get herpes either if I didn't already have it. Instead, the idea of being with me physically was so revolting, he had to claim "friendship"? Like guys ever give a shit about friendship. If a straight guy wants to sleep with you, they sleep with you! Everyone knows that! They basically teach it to you in kindergarten!

Am I so repulsive that the very idea of kissing me makes him resort to his (brief) martial arts background? (I think he took karate as a kid. Who didn't?)

He wanted me to stay so we could "talk about it" and not "make things weird" but I was on the verge of tears, which would only make things *weirder* so I ran away to my room, claiming fatigue and shouting, "Everything is fine! Let's just forget about it!"

As you can now see, I have no choice but to legally change my name and flee the country.

Good-bye forever,

Leena (testing that out as my new fake name)

Re: NOWHERE TO RUN, NOWHERE TO HIDE

 Gen Goldman <GEN.GOLDMAN@gmail.com> 11/10/19

to Ava

Dear Leena (the girl formerly known as Ava),

Holy fuck. That sucks. He elbowed you in the face? Or he just put his elbow in front of his face? Either way. BRUTAL.

I totally understand why you are feeling the way you are feeling. But I do think it's important to point out one thing. Most kids don't do karate. Some kids? Sure. But definitely not most or all.

A second, equally important thing I'd like to say. I AM SO FUCKING PROUD OF YOU! You went for it! You put yourself out there! It didn't go "great" but you are still out there experiencing the highs and lows of being alive. This time it just happened to be a very low low. That's okay! It's all part of the ride!

I also think you assume you've done more damage than you have. Dana seems like a pretty chill dude. This is not the first time in history someone has tried to kiss a friend and it didn't go well. If that was enough to end friendships, I wouldn't have any!

You should take a bit more time to calm down and then go back and face him. I know the easier solution would be to move out or hide when he's home, but you're better than that. You own (rent) half of that living room! Never forget that!

Please keep me updated as the situation develops. And maybe see a doctor about your tea burn.

LOVE YOU LEENA!

GENA (my new fake name)

3:12 PM

 You think I can just waltz back in and act like nothing happened?

I mean, you manage to work with the
guy who gave you herpes so . . . yes?

What do I even say to him?

I would start with hi.

Or maybe a head nod.

That is the craziest thing I have ever
heard.

WHY ARE SOME PEOPLE SO MATURE . . .

Ava Helmer <AVA.HELMER@gmail.com>   11/10/19

to Gen

And why are some people me? Instead of listening to
your advice, I was in the middle of negotiating a hotel
stay using my parents' Starwood points without having
to tell them I wanted to use their Starwood points,
when I got a text from Dana.

DANA: Stop avoiding me and come home.
DANA: I need you to show me how to use the oven.

I don't know how to use the oven, but I do know an
olive branch when it's texted to me. So I tucked my
very damp and sweaty tail between my legs and
headed back to the apartment. I flung open the door
and declared, "I have no idea how to use the oven. I
have never cooked anything in my life."

Dana laughed and told me to google it while he futzed

and thirty-five minutes later we split a Digiorno pizza and talked like adults about "what happened."

I don't understand. Dana is only two months younger than me but infinitely wiser. How is that possible? Are some people just gifted with rational brains the way others are given gorgeous profiles or impeccable math skills? I think if I could wish for one thing it would be a balanced brain. Or *maybe* a better profile. Depends on the day!

Long, mature conversation short, Dana admitted that he had also contemplated the idea of us being more than friends but ultimately decided it wasn't worth the risk. We live together, work together and get along great: as friends. Plus, if we had some undeniable sexual chemistry, wouldn't something have happened between us already?

This was an interesting argument. He was basically suggesting that if our "romantic" feelings for each other were strong enough to risk the friendship, sex (or something physical) would have already happened. Since sex *hadn't* already happened, I was probably confusing platonic feelings of love and affection with romantic feelings of love and affection simply because of convenience and close quarters.

I continue to have NO IDEA if this is true or complete bullshit but it made me reexamine things. Maybe I *don't* have romantic feelings for Dana. Maybe he is just a good friend and confidant and I have never had one of those with male parts before. So I got confused? Or maybe I do have feelings for him, but it doesn't mean they will last. Either way, he isn't going to abruptly leave my life like Ben or any of the other guys I've expressed feelings for. And that feels special. Even if it's platonic special.

Wow. AM I GROWING UP? Probably not. But at least my hives are gone. Did I mention I got hives, which was a redness separate from the tea burn?

Life is life!

Ava-Leena

10:12 PM

Fuck yassss

??

You 2 made up

I guess we were never really in a fight haha, I just freaked out.

makess senseeee

Are you drunk? Or is the cat typing?

Si

It's Sunday night!

You have work tomorrow!

Y DO U THINK I DRINK

EVERYONE SUX

Gen Goldman <GEN.GOLDMAN@gmail.com> 11/11/19
to Ava

I hate this job. I hate Florida. And I hate hangovers. But not as much as I hate Florida.

I showed up to work ON TIME and with one of the best articles I have ever written. That's right. Instead of rushing into Grady's office on Thursday afternoon and demanding he publish a bare-bones transcript of my interview with the mayor, I spent THREE FULL DAYS thinking about what the most effective approach to this material would be. (Well, maybe not three FULL days because I did have that epic threesome/brawl.) But I put a lot of work into this and turned it into somewhat of an op-ed about politicians' reluctance to vocally take a side about controversial situations even though their *actions* reveal how they truly feel. In this case, a refusal to offer support and shelter to the homeless LGBTQ community. It was enlightened, impassioned and, some might say, evocative.

Grady barely skimmed it and then actually said, out loud: "Pass."

Are you fucking kidding me? What sixty-something man says "Pass" out loud?? Does he think he is a judge on *American Idol*?

Apparently, he "doesn't think he is a judge on *American*

Idol" but thinks I need "to focus on actual news and not forcing my personal agenda."

My "personal agenda" is justice and equality for all! I'm sorry if that gets in the way of . . . Actually I have no idea what this could get in the way of, other than someone else's personal agenda. If that agenda is bigotry and inequality.

Grady did not like my attack on his character and sent me home for the day to "rest" since I was "clearly not in any position to do my job."

I think he thought I was on my period! And he could get rid of the problem with a nap and some Midol? WHAT YEAR IS THIS?!

I stormed out of his office, resisting the urge to throw another lamp (hard habit to break) and sped home, crying. Like someone who is actually on their period.

What am I doing here? What am I doing with my life? I bet if I snoop around Grady's office I would find the story of a lifetime. Or at least Grady's lifetime. There is no way that man is clean. Maybe if I take him down they will put someone with a moral compass in charge. Or just shut down this pathetic excuse for a paper.

I'm gonna go burn off some steam at GOTCHA. Here's hoping Coralee isn't there to stick another hole in my gaping metaphorical wound.

Can I bring cats to bars? Don't bother to answer that.
I'm gonna give it a try.

G

2:32 PM

Gen, please tell me you did not bring
your cats to a bar.

Come on. Of course not.

I just brought Tabby.

The kittens are too young to travel.

How many drinks have you had?

58!

No.

85!

Is anyone with you?

I just told you! Tabby!

What's Lyle's number? I think he should
come get you.

Lyle doesn't have a phone.

How does he message Beau all day?

Magic!

Gen. It's 2:30 and you're wasted.

Pshhh. I am fine.

Stop worrying.

You have enough to worry about

???

You're always complaining about
something!

Text me when you're home.

Okay MOM

4:15 PM
 Where are you?

5:47 PM
Asleep.
I know. I found Lyle on Facebook.

8:32 PM
Don't be mad at meeee
I'm not mad.
I'm scared.
Tabby is fine! She's a party animal.
Pun intended as always.
Let's just talk in the morning.
Get some sleep.
UGHHHHHHHHHHH

TWO IDEAS AND A LITTLE LADY

Ava Helmer <AVA.HELMER@gmail.com>   11/12/19
to Gen

Did you ever see that movie *Three Men and a Baby*?
Or the follow-up, *Three Men and a Little Lady*?
Neither have I. But I still know both titles by heart as
well as have a basic idea of what the posters look like.

Why is my brain filled with this useless knowledge instead of brilliant ideas for field pieces to pitch to Halona?

Our ideas are due end of this week.

So far I have:

1) Animals? Why do we love them?

That's it. One of the segment hosts would go visit an animal shelter and try to figure out why we love animals so much without getting distracted by their own overwhelming love of animals.

Maybe I am not meant for late-night television . . .

I think it's pretty obvious my idea isn't gonna get picked and I won't even blame Halona's internalized sexism as the culprit. I'm strangely okay with not getting picked. I hope this is due to maturity and not depression. But I'm not really in a position to be picky either way . . .

I'm feeling more creative when it comes to the YouTube channel. Dana and I have finally decided on our first video: "Why It's Great to Have Herpes—A Satire."

That's right! I'm going public with this (horrible) thing! You were right. I can't keep secrets. Whenever I feel like I have to keep something to myself, a small part of my soul starts to scream: "Tell everyone! Stand up on the subway and tell EVERYONE!" So, to prevent this from happening, I'm going to release this "shameful" information the best way I know how: by making it funny.

I pitched the idea as a joke to Dana during a brainstorming session, but he clung onto it and convinced me it was a great idea. It will be really simple, right-to-camera stuff. Basically a parody of a vlog. He's gonna borrow a camera and we're gonna shoot tonight. I have to figure out what to wear. Something that looks nice but doesn't scream "she was asking for herpes." Any and all suggestions are welcome. Except for nudity.

I am terrified to do this obviously, but I think I am more terrified about what will happen if I don't. Plus, like you've pointed out, all the important people in my life already know and they still love me. Maybe not romantically (cough cough Dana) but I don't feel alone in this. So that's got to count for something right?!

And finally. The little lady part of this whole thing: You. Gen. My bestest friend in this godforsaken world. I am worried about you. And your drinking specifically.

I know you do NOT want to hear this but alcoholism is genetic and you don't have the best family history . . . I'm not saying you need to stop drinking completely right now . . . but I think it's something worth thinking about? Maybe you could set some ground rules?

Like:

1) No drinking during the day.

2) No drinking more than two nights in a row.

3) No more than four drinks at any given time.

4) No drinking alone.

Obviously, I'm just spitballing here. But feel free to use any and all of the above free of charge ;)

Those are my updates/unsolicited thoughts. Please don't be *too* mad at me. I will need your support when the video goes live. Dana wants to disable comments, but that will prevent it from getting any real traction, and if one person feels less alone as a result of my going public, it will be worth it. (Okay, fine, maybe it would need to be at least two.)

Ava Helmer, Professional Herpe-ist

11:27 AM

You're going public????

That is so unbelievably BADASS!

You think so?

I'm so scared!!!

I get that. But you're doing a really great thing for a lot of people!

Visibility is huge.

Yeah but it's not like anyone is going to see the video . . .

The channel has two subscribers and it's just our moms.

What is the channel?! I will subscribe!

It's a bad name.

How? Racist? Sexist? Anti-Semitic?

I'm Jewish!

Oh, and you've never heard of a self-hating Jew?

It's called: "Laugh Hard Now, Cry Harder Later"

That's the channel's name??

I told you it was stupid!

Laugh Now, Cry Later was already taken.

But they don't have any uploads so I think we can still claim the brand.

Hey, I'm into it.

I'm just glad you're making stuff again!

Thank you!!!

How's work?

I dunno.

?

I'm at home.

Taking a "personal day."

Are you drinking?

The number you have dialed is no longer in service.

Gen! It's not even noon!

That's why I'm also having orange juice! For a balanced meal!

BACKUP CAREERS

 Gen Goldman <GEN.GOLDMAN@gmail.com> 11/12/19

to Ava

1) Phlebotomist. Involves years of schooling but I would get to say the word *phlebotomist* at least once a day.

2) Used Car Salesman. We both know I can lie circles around Trump. Might as well put this skill to good use instead of wasting it by focusing on "journalistic integrity."

3) Cam Girl. For the money. And the stories.

4) Professional Groupie. I think if I pick the right band this could be very lucrative . . . I could sell merch and save money on rent by sleeping in a van.

5) Trophy Wife. We both know I clean up good.

Right now I'm leaning towards 4 but I can be persuaded towards 1 if you pay for my schooling.

Gen, Future Phlebotomist*

*Say that ten times fast. It'll be a lot of fun!

Re: BACKUP CAREERS

Ava Helmer <AVA.HELMER@gmail.com>   11/12/19
to Gen

What about a journalist who just doesn't live in
Florida??

WE'RE LIVE BABY!!

Ava Helmer <AVA.HELMER@gmail.com>   11/13/19
to Gen

Dana and I stayed up until 2 in the morning editing.
(Well, Dana hit the buttons but I stayed awake! Which
is a feat unto itself!)

I think it came out great! The right mix of facts and
funny. I don't think I'm ready to be a professional actor,
but I'm pretty good at being sarcastic. Who knew? (That
was sarcastic.) We uploaded at 10AM EST to maximize
views (haha). At least twelve people have watched it!

The only downside (so far) was my parents' reaction.
They're both pretty shocked I went public with my
"condition" and not so subtly urged me to take it down
before too many people see. My dad thinks it might get
in the way of me having a "normal career." I don't know
how having herpes will negatively affect my career

unless he thinks I'm going to sleep with everyone I
work with and get fired for infecting them????

I guess I *did* sleep with Ben, which is what got me into
this whole mess. So maybe he does have a point.

I HATE upsetting my parents but I'm really proud of the
video. Maybe if it gets some positive feedback they will
come around?

Dana is sending it out to pretty much everyone he has
ever met, which is a surprising number of people
considering we spend like 80 percent of our time
together. Maybe he has a secret life after I go to bed?

I'm most excited for you to watch! I hope you like it!!!

Are you back at work today?

Xoxox

A

11:49 AM
Ahhhh!
I LOVE it!!
Really????
REALLY! It's so sad and funny!
It was mostly meant to be funny . . .
Maybe it's just sad because I know you?
I don't know if that makes it better or
worse.

Can I post it?

Where?

Everywhere!!!

Maybe just not FB. Too many old teachers friended me.

FB is dead anyway.

I also think Zuckerberg has been dead for years and replaced by a clone.

I know you think that. You tweet about it all the time.

Don't hate the players, hate the organization.

Are you at work?

Yes, I'm at work, Mom.

Am I doing work? That's another story.

I'm just glad you're not dead in a ditch.

2:58 PM

Oh fuck.

Ben wants "to talk."

If you take that A-hole back I will beat you.

And then support your choice to ruin your life.

Because I'm pro-choice in all situations.

Get it?

I really don't think he wants to get back together.

He looks mad . . .

I AM A SURVIVOR . . .

 Ava Helmer <AVA.HELMER@gmail.com> 11/13/19
to Gen

Of gaslighting. I think I finally understand that term!
And the type of horrible people who try to inflict it.

My intuition about Ben was spot-on. I know it's not
possible for steam to come out of someone's ears, but
I think his rage actually radiated heat.

He grabbed me after an all-staff meeting where Halona
played us some of her favorite YouTube videos. Half of
them were just clips from *SNL* . . . Needless to say I
have a very important job (Internship).

We went to grab a coffee around the corner but before
I could even order, he dug into me.

BEN: Did you just do it to get back at me? Because
that's pretty immature.
AVA: Did I just do *what* to get back at you? Caramel
Macchiato please!

hold for ordering

BEN: You know what, Ava. The video.

Full disclosure, I did know what but I wanted to
make him have to explain so he could dig his own
hole.

AVA: That video has nothing to do with you. It doesn't even mention you.
BEN: But people know we dated!
AVA: So?
BEN: Now people will think *I* have herpes.
AVA: You DO have herpes! Or do you genuinely keep forgetting? Maybe that's why you forgot to tell me before we slept together.
BEN: I don't know who is putting you up to this, but petty doesn't look good on you.

ARE YOU KIDDING ME?!!! Where is he getting his insults from? A 1950's guide to disarming housewives? Totally honestly: it stung . . . but they were mean back then.

After five minutes of me somewhat calmly explaining not everything I do has to do with him, Ben changed tactics.

BEN: Are you worried? About everyone knowing? You're just starting out. It could get in the way of stuff.
AVA: Would you not hire someone because they have a completely contained infection that is only sometimes contagious through sexual contact?
BEN: Not me, personally, but people are weird about this stuff. It's better to keep it private—
AVA: From your sexual partners?
BEN: I get it. You're pissed I didn't tell you. But doesn't that just prove my point? It's not a cool thing to have and I don't think you really thought through the entire world knowing your business.
AVA: You're right. I probably didn't "think it through." I got caught up in the excitement of making something

and taking back control over my life and my shame.
But now that you are making me look at it from all
sides . . . I'm really glad I did it. Because people
shouldn't be censored by shame.

Okay, maybe I wasn't THAT articulate in the moment.
But I think I got my main point across, which was
FUCK YOU. The video is staying up. I then walked out
without him and when I got to my desk we suddenly
had ten thousand views?? I don't know how. But I will
definitely take it.

AM I A VIRAL SENSATION?

A

8:38 PM

35,923!

Views???

Yep! And I am only responsible for like
fifty of them!

This is so cool!

Now my former teachers definitely know
I have herpes!

When you think about the poor sex
education in this country, it's technically
their fault . . .

I really don't know if my former Latin
instructor will see it that way but I can
certainly hope!

Thank you for making me do this!

Or giving me the courage to do it!

Anytime babe ;)

I told you to stop calling me babe.

You got it, toots.

Thu, Nov 14, 3:45 AM

I took my own advice!!

🙌🙌🙌🙌

6:50 AM

Oh no.

What does that mean???

Why were you awake at 3:45???

GEN!!!!

8:27 AM

Hola!

What did you do?!

I took my own advice!

You married a foreign oil magnate and sold all his company shares to Greenpeace for one dollar??

No! That advice only applied to Kelly because that oil guy wanted to marry her.

So what did you do?

Blackmail your landlord into giving you cheaper rent by using his tax evasion against him?

No! That was just advice for Alex when he was living in Boston!

But you can see why I'm worried, right?

Not the best track record.

If either of them had LISTENED to my advice, I'm sure they'd be a lot better off than they are now.

Kelly is happily engaged to her college BF!

They're already ENGAGED?!

We're barely baby adults! What is wrong with straight people?!

STOP STRAIGHT PEOPLE DEFLECTING!

WHAT DID YOU DO?!!

I stopped waiting on other people to accomplish what I want professionally.

Which means . . .

I posted the interview with the mayor to the website without Grady's permission 😎

What??

Won't you get in big trouble for that?!

Too early to tell.

OY!

HOW THE MIGHTY HAVE FALLEN

 Gen Goldman <GEN.GOLDMAN@gmail.com> 11/14/19

to Ava

So . . . I got fired. Not laid off. Or downsized. Or relocated to my home without pay. Straight up FIRED. Feels a little dramatic, no?

I showed up to work relatively on time. I mean I was up until 4AM hacking the website from my personal computer (sorry, intern Cash!) so I figured I could let myself sleep in a bit. But I didn't even make it to my desk before Grady bellowed my name.

After an epic sigh, I joined him in his office.

GRADY: I assume you know why you're in here?
GEN: Nope.
GRADY: So you didn't upload an unapproved article to the website last night?
GEN: No, I did that. But I wasn't sure if that's why I was in here.

unofficial stare down that I unofficially win

GRADY: Why would you do something like this?
GEN: Well, I am here to report the news. And I felt it was my journalistic duty to cover this story to the best of my ability. Also, I was under the impression you never even looked at the website.
GRADY: Of course I look at the website!
GEN: Really?

GRADY: Not every day, but I certainly check it out when I get a concerned call from the mayor's office at 7AM!

GEN: The mayor reads *The Fernandina Beach Centennial* online?

GRADY: I don't know. But he certainly reads Google Alerts.

GEN: Ohhh. Google Alerts. I forgot about those.

GRADY: What was your plan here? For no one to read the article? What's the point of that?

GEN: I thought it would gain traction on some liberal outlets and social media so by the time you found out about it, you couldn't take it down without getting backlash.

Grady takes his glasses off and rubs his eyes. I notice I cause this reaction in a lot of people

GRADY: That's smart—

GEN: Thank you.

GRADY: But it didn't work. And now I need to suspend you. Without pay.

GEN: Suspend me?! I'm the only one at the office that does anything.

GRADY: That's not fair or true.

GEN: Oh really?! When was the last time Phyllis uncovered anything? And Beau spends all his time talking to his fake girlfriend—

GRADY: What fake girlfriend?

So this is where I might have gone off the rails a bit. I was groggy from lack of sleep and maybe one too many beers. (I had four beers, okay? But spread out.)

I guess I will never know why, but I told Grady everything. About Beulah and Lyle and Beau's obsession. Halfway through he called Beau into the office and made me tell him everything. That did not go well.

BEAU: So it's been you this whole time?
GEN: Well, me and Lyle. Mostly Lyle.
BEAU: Who is Lyle?!
GEN: Lyle Rainbow? From the Open All Doors piece?
BEAU: I've been talking with a dude??? A GAY dude??
GEN: He's gay, yeah, but has a very feminine aura—
BEAU: Why would you do this??
GEN: You seemed lonely.
BEAU: You think you did this to HELP me?

I shrug

GEN: Haven't you been happier lately?
BEAU: I'm not happy right now!

Grady interrupted at this point to stop what I can only imagine would have become a "rumble." He said in light of my recent harassment and bullying(?) he had no choice but to fire me. I was given five minutes to exit the premises. Before I left, I made sure to give them the login details for the website and made them promise not to fire Cash. Grady thanked me and told me he'd be sure to change them. Smartest decision he's made in a while.

Anyway, I'm fired! So now I'm not just in debt. I'm unemployed and in debt. Maybe I can work at

GOTCHA? They are always unbearably understaffed.
Or maybe their staff is just unbearably slow. Either way
I'll ask about job openings once I finish this drink.

How's your video doing??

G

1:32 PM

GEN!

I just saw your email!

Are you okay???

Golden!

Does that mean okay??

hahaha I'm fine!

People get fired all the time.

What are you gonna do? Move back
home?

FUCK no!

The only place worse than this shithole
is anywhere with my parents.

Okay. Maybe you could move here?

OH MY GOD!!!! MOVE HERE????

I can't afford New York, Ava.

No one can afford New York! That's part
of the fun!

Can you give me like four hours of
enjoying my freedom before forcing me
to plan my future??

Yes. Absolutely. Sorry

1:41 PM

Are you drinking?

6:23 PM

Watch my story!

On Instagram?

DUH!

6:26 PM

Gen!

That's dangerous!

Relax! I know how to swim!

Whose boat is that??

A new friend.

I think you should go home for the night.
Get some rest.

Rest is for losers!

I rest all the time!

Exactly ;)

WORRIED ABOUT YOU

 Ava Helmer <AVA.HELMER@gmail.com>   11/14/19
to Gen

That's pretty much it. I'm here if you need me. I'm here
even if you think you don't. Getting fired is a scary

horrible thing. Even if you didn't like the job in the first place.

Please don't self-destruct. You're the only one I can tolerate in small, medium or large doses.

Love always,

Ava

P.S. The video has 57K views now! I can only assume you did something with your magic fingers. (Like posting it on Reddit.)

Fri, Nov 15, 8:27 AM
Good morning!!!

9:52 AM
Hellooooo!!!

1:12 PM
It is the afternoon!

1:23 PM
I'm up.
How'd you sleep??

Harumph.

Remember to drink water 🖤

6:57 PM

How was your day?

Thrilling. I slept and then went back to sleep.

That sounds an awful lot like depression. Do you feel depressed?

It's been ONE day! Leave me alone!

Sorry! Sorry!

Let me know if you want help filling out unemployment paperwork. I've heard it can be pretty tricky.

ONE DAY!

Sorry.

GOOD MORNING, YOU DARK CLOUD!!

Ava Helmer <AVA.HELMER@gmail.com>   11/16/19
to Gen

So I've been asking around, and it turns out Lacie's roommate works at this women-only work space downtown and they are hiring people to run a newsletter. I know it's not your typical print journalism but they're exclusively hiring people with a journalism background to write about women's issues in New York??? Could be, I don't know, PERFECT?!

Plus, you could probably do freelance work on the side to supplement the income? I talked to Dana and you are more than welcome to crash on our couch until you find a place of your own. You just have to promise to not sleep with Dana. I know I will never sleep with Dana, and I have made my peace with that, but I think I would lose it if you slept with him. Even if it was "casual and didn't mean anything." I am petty and weak and I appreciate your sexual restraint at this time.

Anyway, here is the email to send your resume: harperopenings@gmail.com

Let me know what you think of this plan!! I think it is my best plan of all time!

A

P.S. I can't wait for you to move here and find/show me all the places I should have been going this whole time!

3:17 PM

Alex thinks he can probably get me a job at ACORE. It would be super entry level, but I guess the pay is good.

Did you get my email???

Yeah.

And?!

I can't move to New York, Ava.

It's too expensive.

But so is D.C. . . . .

But I would have a job in D.C.

You could have a job in New York!

And you wouldn't even have to pay rent at first because you could stay with me and my herpes.

I'm sure I could stay with Alex too.

You don't even care about green energy! I've never seen you recycle!

That's not true! I do it whenever there is a sign.

Do you not want to live near me? Is that what this is about?

oh my god Ava

Not everything is about you.

HI MY NAME IS GEN . . .

 Gen Goldman <GEN.GOLDMAN@gmail.com> 11/18/19

to Ava

And I like to self-sabotage.

You probably do not find this surprising since you have seen me do it a countless amount of times. Another thing I love to do is lash out at the ones who love me the most, which at this point, is pretty much you.

After getting fired (and honestly before) I fell into something of a black hole. I was mad at everyone and everything. I was also pretty pissed that I don't have any sort of safety cushion. Like if my parents were financially responsible AT ALL I wouldn't have to worry about ending up on the street. But, instead, they're morons and the only person looking out for me financially is me. And we both know I am not good at finances. Some might say, I am very bad at finances. I don't even want to tell you how much I have spent on custom cat costumes that they all refuse to wear. (Over $200. As in, over $300. On a credit card.)

I would never begrudge your parents or your background, but shit like this makes me a little resentful because it will just never be the same for you. Getting fired isn't just embarrassing. It's terrifying. So I didn't want to face all of that. So I drank instead. And then being hungover makes me extra cranky so I drink more . . .

And I get why my drinking freaks you out. It freaks me out too. I don't want to end up like my dad. But I'm also twenty-two and I don't think I need to be sober for my entire life because I'm afraid of what *might* happen. I can handle myself and I also promise to wait until at least noon to crack one open. Unless I'm at brunch. There are no rules at brunch.

I'm thinking of going back to some Al-Anon meetings. I went to some in college and they helped me with "my anger issues." I don't know. I sort of need to focus on the whole "employment" thing before rooting around in my damaged past.

Anywayyyy I'm sorry I was a dick. I spent the entire weekend drinking my sorrows and trying to get Alex to flirt with me. I was this close to doing something really drastic like driving to Mexico or I don't know, maybe heroin, when something incredible happened.

Beau walked into my house. Yep, that Beau. I sprang up from my sinkhole of depression (the couch) and prepared for a proper beating. I figured I had like a 15 percent shot of being too drunk to feel the pain. But then Lyle walked in behind him. Turns out they were going to go to a movie after getting some coffee and Lyle wanted to grab a jacket.

Before your heart starts to do a gay flutter: I have to warn you. This is not a love story. But it *is* a friendship story. Apparently, after I let the cat out of the bag and exposed Beulah as a scam, Lyle reached out to Beau from his personal account. He explained how much he had enjoyed their conversations, and even though Beau must feel betrayed, everything Lyle said was true (you know, other than all the stuff about Beulah).

I guess Beau wrote back and suggested they meet up in person to put a face to a fake name. So they went to coffee and now they're friends? I think this is the first time in a long time I have faith in humanity?

It also made me realize that I've been an exceptionally shitty person lately and you deserve an apology.

I also applied to the NY job so you would stop bugging me about it.

Cross your fingers and toes. Nothing would make me happier than sleeping on your couch.

G

HI MY NAME IS AVA . . .

 Ava Helmer <AVA.HELMER@gmail.com>   11/18/19
to Gen

And I am happy crying right now. Thank you for your email and thank you for apologizing! It feels like Christmas! Or some other holiday that I actually celebrate.

I'm sorry things have been so shitty for you. And I am always a bit behind when it comes to finance stuff. But I honestly think we can make N.Y. work together. If you eat a street dog twice a day, you're basically surviving on next to nothing! (Also dollar pizza! It's everywhere!) And you don't have to live in Manhattan. We both know you're more Williamsburg or Bushwick than mainland. (Do people call Manhattan "mainland"? I think they should!)

Re: drinking. I'll keep my mouth shut . . . for now. But I do fully support this Al-Anon idea and will do my best to never invite you to brunch. Seems like only bad things will happen if we brunch.

And now for the main event: LYLE AND BEAU!!!!! Oh my god!!! That is so cute and wonderful!! Imagine if they become best friends just like us?? Your catfish turned into a real mitzvah! I did NOT see that coming!

I'm sorry it took me until tonight to respond. A crazy thing happened on Friday and now I am producing my own segment for *Mind the Gap* so I actually had work to do today!

Still crying,

A

9:13 PM

I got your own segment???!!?!!

Why didn't you tell me!?

I don't know! 🙈

Did it have anything to do with me being fired?

Maybe????

Ava! You can always share your good news with me!

Even when I'm being a bitch!

Hahaha OK

Noted for the future!

So Halona liked the shelter dog pitch??

God no.

No one liked that.

???

They went with a different one.

I'll email you tomorrow!

About to watch Dana perform indie improv

Wow.

@ Sending you the strength to not fall
asleep.

@ Thank you. I'll need it.

WHEN LIFE GIVES YOU HERPES . . .

Ava Helmer <AVA.HELMER@gmail.com>   11/19/19
to Gen

Use it to advance your career?

I showed up to the all-staff intern pitch meeting on
Friday already embarrassed for my future self. I wasn't
as prepared as I should have been, and even though
animals are great, no one wants to cover them on
late-night unless a politician was caught fondling a bear.
(Do you think it's even *possible* to fondle a bear?
Animal sexual organs remain a mystery to me.) I sat in
the back and hoped Halona would lose interest in her
own idea before I got to share mine. This has happened
many times before. She once asked for each segment
producer to make a video presentation of their own
lives and then left during the first one for an "important
appointment." It's one thing to walk out on someone's
idea . . . it's another to walk out on someone's life!

When Halona walked in with a smile and a Venti Latte,
my stomach dropped. People started murmuring.
There had been much discussion of cutting her
down to Grandes only. The last time she had a Venti
Latte the staff meeting went from 10 to 11. As in 10AM

to **11PM**. Thankfully, that was before my time. I would have had to quit around 9PM.

Anywho, she walked in, talking a mile a minute and I felt my whole body clench up. There was no way I was going to make it through the meeting without having to eventually talk. Just as I worried about having to speak, I HEARD myself speaking. Out of the loudspeakers. Haloma was playing my herpes video on the TV. I had no idea what was happening.

The only explanations that made any sense were:

1) Elaborate prank

2) Alternate dimension

3) Trapped in a dream

So, since this clearly wasn't reality, I let myself sit back and enjoy the (false) moment. People seemed to really like the video. Everyone was laughing. A lot of people looked at me and smiled. Except Ben. Ben was scowling. But why was Ben scowling in my dream? My unconscious mind can't even fabricate a truly blissful experience—and then it hit me. I was conscious and this was all real.

HALONA MCBRIDE WAS PLAYING MY VIDEO ON THE TV IN FRONT OF THE ENTIRE STAFF! AND PEOPLE WERE LAUGHING!

I finally understood that this WAS happening. But I didn't understand WHY it was happening. Until the video finished and Halona announced I would be producing a segment on STDs for the intern field piece. Before she could explain anything else, she hit her head on one of the lamps and left the room, pissed off.

Everyone stared at me, unsure of what to do. No one else had had the opportunity to pitch their ideas. I hadn't even had the chance to formally pitch an idea. I felt the tides of envy turning but then Dana started a slow clap. That turned into a real clap and before I knew it, people were congratulating me! And it seemed to be sincere! (For the most part.)

A couple people also told me they "knew someone" with herpes. Not sure what I'm supposed to do with that information . . .

And then the meeting was adjourned. Shayna, that junior producer who just got bumped up to segment producer, offered to help me navigate the piece SINCE I HAVE NO IDEA WHAT I'M DOING!

I brainstormed all weekend and I think I landed on an interview with an abstinence-only educator. The hook will be something along the lines of me revealing I have herpes, the educator trying to shame me about it, and then me not letting them? I'm not sure. It's a work in progress. I have until the end of this week to figure it out.

So that is my big, huge, unbelievable update! I'm sorry I didn't tell you right away but I was trying to be considerate yadda yadda.

Give Tabby and the threesome a kiss from me!

Ava

2:47 PM

I french-kissed all four cats in your honor!

Aw! Thank you!

Please never do that again.

Sorry! Got too much free time not to at least experiment.

I'm worried you know too much about animals' sexual organs.

Congrats on your segment! It's gonna be amazing!!!

Or very bad!

Could go either way!

Nah.

That's only true about most people's sexual orientations.

9:16 PM

I'm very impressed you haven't inquired about my "next steps."

It must be killing you.

Why do you think I haven't texted?!!

I'm trying to respect your process!

Of being unemployed?

Of FINDING yourself.

Fuck. That's what I'm supposed to be doing?

Or applying to jobs in N.Y. either way!

What am I supposed to do with my lease?

It's not like I have credit score to spare.

Sublet it to Lyle!

Lyle is homeless.

Not if he sublets your apartment!

9:27 PM

Is it illegal for me to apply for jobs in your name?

Not sure if it's illegal but it's psychotic!

Psychotic has never stopped me before!

What is your social security number?

123-45-6789

Perfect!

WHO AM I, WHAT AM I

 Gen Goldman <GEN.GOLDMAN@gmail.com> 11/20/19
to Ava

That's what Dr. Seuss should have named at least one of his books! I might have actually read it . . . (Please do not suggest actual self-help books to me right now. I'm not that far gone.)

It is a very strange thing to wake up and have no purpose. I thought this would feel like an unpaid vacation, but stress has already settled in and I'm worried about . . . my future? Is this why adults are in bad moods all of the time?

I finally returned my mother's call this morning after two weeks of ignoring texts (aka spiritual memes). She started grilling me about work and I told her we had "respectfully parted ways." I thought she'd act shocked or disappointed but she just sighed and asked if I needed money!

First of all, they don't have any money! What was she going to do if I said yes? Tell me to take out a loan!? Why does she insist on pretending she can fulfill any sort of parental role in my life? Is it a pride thing? I bet it's a pride thing. (Fucking genetics.)

Second, did she ASSUME I was going to get fired? Or part ways? Or whatever the fuck I told her? I was editor-in-chief of *The Berkeley Beacon*! I am a (student) award-winning journalist! I am going to make something of myself, whether they read about it or not.

So now I can't even enjoy my couch nap because I feel like a failure. I need a job ASAP. But I also need a career long-term.

UGH! Why did I have to be born with this free-loving personality AND ambition?!

It's a curse.

G

P.S. Thank god for having great legs. They are an uncomplicated gift.

P.P.S. Beau got Lyle a job working at some family friend's restaurant. Apparently he is going to make *bank* in tips. At least I enriched both of their lives while ruining my own. And if I ever find my way out of here I have someone to sublet my place. (Does this count as a silver lining if it is mostly good news for someone else?)

P.P.P.S. I should never have gone to college. (Because of the student loans. The nightlife was awesome.)

3:48 PM

It's only been one week!

You will find your purpose!

You would freak out after one day if you got fired.

Sure. But I have generalized anxiety disorder.

I freak out if I'm running on time instead of early.

Wow. You're so weird.

I feel better.

9:12 PM

Dana just kissed me!

OH MY GOD! REALLY?!!!

Nope!

I'm just trying to prank more.

Good one?

There's a learning curve . . .

10:23 PM

Maybe I should go into space.

Sure! Follow your dreams!

Then we'd be really far from each other . . .

I take it back!

Follow my dreams!

AHHHHHHHHHHHHHHHH!

Ava Helmer <AVA.HELMER@gmail.com>   11/21/19

to Gen

I don't think my video makes any sense. I think I need to rethink the entire idea. What if I went to an STD clinic instead? Or, what if I somehow brought the abstinence educator to an STD clinic with me? What is my angle? What am I trying to say??

I can't believe I'm getting this amazing break and I'm going to fuck it up.

Re: AHHHHHHHHHHHHHHH!

Ava Helmer <AVA.HELMER@gmail.com>   11/21/19

to Gen

I figured it out! I think it's going to be really good!
Probably the best thing I've ever done.

Re: AHHHHHHHHHHHHHHH!

Gen Goldman <GEN.GOLDMAN@gmail.com> 11/21/19

to Ava

Happy to help!

HOW MUCH FAILURE IS TOO MUCH FAILURE??

Gen Goldman <GEN.GOLDMAN@gmail.com> 11/21/19

to Ava

I know we're in our early twenties and we're allowed to
"figure stuff out" until most of our high school
class gets married or knocked up, but at what point
am I just a loser who doesn't have her life together?

Yes, I got myself fired. Not for being bad at my job but
for being too much of myself. But what if myself isn't

good at having a job? What if I just float from one mediocre opportunity to another and suddenly I'm middle-aged and still cohabitating with a random person to save on rent? I have a brain! I should be allowed to use it to make cash!

Maybe I should go to Grady and beg for my job back. There is no way he'll give it to me but his wife might need a housekeeper or something?!

I feel like I want to break up with myself. You know, "It's not me, it's you who is also me."

Wow. I'm so sad. Is this what it's like to be you?

G

Re: HOW MUCH FAILURE IS TOO MUCH FAILURE??

 Ava Helmer <AVA.HELMER@gmail.com>   11/21/19
to Gen

Hello.

I have very mixed feelings about this email because:

1) I'm so proud of you for thinking about the future! I never thought I'd see the day.

2) I'm devastated that you think you are a failure. Gen, you are the most talented, vivacious and interesting

person I know. Your path might not be straight (pun intended) but I know it will be filled with adventure and success.

3) I don't feel that sad anymore! Am I cured??? Or do I just have even further to fall???

If I had to whittle all of those feelings down into one response it would be: ONLY GO FORWARD. DO NOT GO BACK.

Grady is out of your life. *The Fernandina Beach Centennial* is out of your life. You are destined for greater things. Just make yourself open to new opportunities and don't be afraid to chase them. There is nothing embarrassing about not getting what you want. I think it's more embarrassing to not want anything in the first place.

Also, move to New York. PLEASE.

A

P.S. I guess you don't *have* to move here. You can still go to space.

2:47 PM

What is your address?

Why?! Are you going to send me something?!

You don't need to send me something!

You should be saving money!

I'm not sending you anything.

Oh.

Then why do you need my address?

So I know where to go after my interview.

At the work space???

Yep. They just called to set up a time.

OH MY GOD!

When is it?!

Tomorrow.

I lied and said I live in Brooklyn.

AHHHHHHHHHHHHHH

This is the best news I've ever heard!

I feel like I just got engaged!

See, that kind of thing is why people think our friendship is weird.

Fuck those people!

WE'RE GONNA BE ROOMMATES!

3:12 PM

Remember three hours ago when you thought you were a failure?!!

Life is wild.

Fri, Nov 22, 9:27 AM

I just landed.

I know!

How?? I didn't even tell you my flight number.

I figured it out.

I'm at baggage claim.

YOU'RE AT THE AIRPORT????

Don't you have a job??

Or did you get fired too???

I took a "sick" day!

My moral compass is getting more flexible.

I can't believe you're here!

Are you sure you're not "in love" in love with me?

Pretty sure!

But I miss you so much we can kiss if you want!

AHHH!

I can't wait to get off the motherfuckin plane!

9:42 AM

We are still waiting for a gate.

That's okay! I'm reading memes!

Reading memes? Do people say that?

I do!

10:01 AM

If the airport goes under lockdown, it's because I tried to blow up this plane.

Don't joke about that!!!!!

I want them to read it! So they will escort me off this plane and into your loving arms.

I can't hug you in jail. Too many germs.

10:09 AM

We got a gate!

I have stood up!

Good for you!

You're at baggage claim?

Yep! Just me and this driver who has told me his whole life story even though I won't make eye contact.

I love New York!

10:15 AM

I don't see you.

Where are you?

Where are you?

I'm by baggage claim 5.

Oh.

I'm not.

Could use more info . . .

This terminal only has four baggage claims . . .

No. It has five.

LOOK BEHIND YOU

AHHHHHHH!

You look great!! Herpes agrees with you!

SHUT UP AND HUG ME

EPILOGUE

DECEMBER SOMETHING

6:45 PM

Hello. Can you please wash your dishes?
I think they are growing mold.

Yeah. Yeah. Sorry.

Work has been crazy.

I work too, you know.

Why, yes you do, Ms. Junior Producer.

Speaking of, when is Dana getting the
rest of his stuff?

How is that speaking of? He doesn't
work with me anymore.

I know. But I'm really sick of all his stuff
lying around. Can you text him?

Fine.

When you do the dishes.

Fine.

6:55 PM

Wanna get takeout and watch a movie tonight?!

I already ordered the food and picked a movie . . .

Perfect! I hate making decisions.

See ya soon!

See ya soon!

ACKNOWLEDGMENTS

First and foremost to our biggest champion (and manager), Matt Sadeghian. We would be much less successful without you. Huge thank-you to our fearless editor, Sara Goodman, who has given us not one but TWO huge opportunities. Shout-out to Sasha Raskin, for getting this whole thing started. We bow down to Ella Dawson, for consulting on the book. And finally, thank you to both our families, who have shaped us into whatever it is we are now. Love you guys.